"This is .... my
life," H...

Kelly felt his frustration to her core. "Tell me about it." She picked at a piece of lint on her slacks, begging her mind to drift to something besides their wedding. In only a matter of moments, they'd left their small town and were heading toward Wilmington. "So, where are we going tonight?"

"It's a bit of a surprise." Harold placed his hand on her knee. "Would you mind if we didn't go see a movie tonight?"

Kelly felt a smile bowing her lips. She lifted her hand to one of her silver earrings and twisted it around her fingertips. "We're not going racecar driving, are we? I'm way overdressed for that."

Harold laughed and tapped the top of the steering wheel. "No racecar driving tonight."

JENNIFER JOHNSON and her unbelievably supportive husband, Albert, are happily married and raising Brooke, Hayley, and Allie, the three cutest young ladies on the planet. Besides being a middle school teacher, Jennifer loves to read, write, and chauffeur her girls. She is a member of American Christian Fiction Writers. Blessed beyond measure, Jennifer hopes to always think like a child—bigger than imaginable and with complete faith. Send her a note at jenwrites4god@bellsouth.net.

Books by Jennifer Johnson

HEARTSONG PRESENTS
HP725—By His Hand
HP738—Picket Fence Pursuit
HP766—Pursuing the Goal
HP802—In Pursuit of Peace
HP866—Finding Home

For Better
or Worse

Jennifer Johnson

Heartsong Presents

This book is dedicated to my mother, Susan Miles. I am thankful for her love for God and desire to always be in the center of His will. Mom, I will always be thankful that you were such a good mom during my "Zoey" years.

A note from the Author:
I love to hear from my readers! You may correspond with me by writing:

Jennifer Johnson
Author Relations
PO Box 721
Uhrichsville, OH 44683

ISBN 978-1-60260-679-1

FOR BETTER OR WORSE

Scripture taken from the HOLY BIBLE, NEW INTERNATIONAL VERSION®. NIV®. Copyright © 1973, 1978, 1984 by International Bible Society. Used by permission of Zondervan. All rights reserved.

All of the characters and events in this book are fictitious. Any resemblance to actual persons, living or dead, or to actual events is purely coincidental.

Our mission is to publish and distribute inspirational products offering exceptional value and biblical encouragement to the masses.

PRINTED IN THE U.S.A.

one

Kelly Coyle gazed around the room at the collection of family members who'd come to celebrate her day. Her mother, though in her midsixties and battling arthritis, still dyed her hair a dark brown, wore makeup to perfection, clothes that would look trendy on a thirty-year-old, and acted every bit as spry as Kelly ever could. Her father, with his salt-and-pepper hair and the most amazing, strike-you-down, blue eyes she'd ever seen, sat on the carpet beside her mother's chair. Kelly's young niece, Ellie, had both of them immersed in a dog and cat puzzle the second grader had brought with her.

Kelly's sister-in-law's laughter sounded from the kitchen. Kelly knew her brother, Cam, was in there with her. There was no telling what shenanigans the two of them planned to pull for Kelly's thirty-eighth birthday.

Kelly's gaze turned to her three daughters. Somehow they had ended up sitting on the couch in stair-step order. Zoey, seventeen, her firstborn, sat with her legs crossed, elbow planted into the armrest and her chin plopped into the palm of her hand. Her appearance had undergone a marked transformation in the last three years—darker hair, darker makeup, darker clothes. Since Tim died, everything about Zoey had darkened.

Tall, thin, athletic, always-trying-to-please, fifteen-year-old Brittany sat in the middle of the couch. The middle child. Brittany second-guessed herself regarding every decision she made. She proved quick to follow others, and there were times Kelly grew more concerned about her follow-the-leader mentality than Zoey's rebellious attitude.

Candy sat cross-legged beside Brittany. Even though she was eleven and going into middle school in a few short weeks, Candy could not sit still. She was energetic, busy, and always into everyone else's business. She had to be the center of everything and everyone knew it. But her heart glowed as genuine as her body was active, and many a day God had used her youngest to give Kelly the motivation to keep going after Tim's death.

"Penny for your thoughts."

Kelly looked up at the man who'd whispered in her ear. Harold Smith, her knight in shining armor. In reality, he was more like the heating guy carrying the wrench, but he'd still saved the day. And after that he'd continued to bless her life. So many people struggle to find a godly love once, and yet God had blessed her twice. She smiled up at his expectant gaze. "I was thinking about how good God has been to me. What a blessing my family is."

"I agree." Harold leaned closer, gently pressing his lips against hers. It was cliché, something she could hear her high schoolers say or write in their short stories for her junior/senior language arts class, but the truth was that electricity still shot through her veins when that man's lips touched hers.

Harold stood to his full height, and Kelly caught a glimpse of Zoey's contemptuous expression. Kelly released a slow sigh. Tim had been gone for three years, and Kelly hadn't started dating Harold until almost a year ago. She'd dated no one else, but Kelly knew Zoey's bitterness wasn't directed at Harold. The teen had never gotten past Tim's car accident.

She'd never made peace with God. Kelly picked up her glass from the end table and took a slow drink. Every day Kelly prayed Zoey would embrace God's peace.

Candy jumped off the couch, breaking Kelly's reverie. She walked to Kelly and put one arm around her shoulder then twirled a lock of her own hair around the thumb and index finger of her free hand. "Do you feel like an old lady now, Mommy?"

Kelly gulped her soft drink in an attempt not to spew it all over the floor. She wiped her mouth with a napkin as laughter burst from her gut. A chorus of guffaws sounded from the family. "Thirty-eight isn't that old."

Candy's cheeks flushed as the preteen furrowed her brows in embarrassment. It was apparent she didn't understand the response of the adults. Candy stammered, "But Sara's mom is only thirty-four, and Tabitha's mom is twenty-nine." She scrunched her nose. "I guess Tabitha's mom is the youngest mom in my class. But thirty-eight is the oldest. I don't know anybody else's mom who is that old."

Kelly wrapped her arms around her youngest child. "But I look good, right?"

"Huh?" Candy scrunched her nose.

Kelly released a laugh as she kissed the top of Candy's head. "You always make my day."

Harold grabbed Candy's hand, his lips tightly pinched in an obvious effort not to laugh. "Come on, you little flatterer, help me get your mom's cake."

Candy's face lit up. "All right." She pulled away from Kelly's embrace. "What's a flatterer, Harold? Why did everyone laugh at me? They're always laughing at me, and I don't know what I do that is so funny."

Kelly watched as the twosome made their way into the kitchen. Candy and Brittany had taken to Harold in only a matter of weeks. Zoey was a different story, but then she wasn't even fond of Kelly anymore. Harold looked back and winked, making her heart race. Three years ago, she would have never dreamed she would feel this way about another man.

When her husband and father of her three daughters died in a car accident, Kelly thought she'd never know happiness again. As time passed, God began to heal her pain and she was able to enjoy life—her family, her friends, her church, her students. Contentment was the appropriate word to describe what she felt before she met Harold. At peace with herself and her situation.

Then her heater quit working.

The memory brought a smile to her lips. Her brother, Cam, had taken care of all their repair needs after Tim died. Electrical problems. Plumbing issues. Whatever needed fixed, Cam did it. But last November, Cam, his wife, Sadie, and their daughter, Ellie, had taken a short trip to visit her parents in Washington. When Kelly's heater gurgled its last, Kelly believed she and the girls would tough it out until Cam returned. Until the temperature in the house plunged to fifty degrees. Kelly had no choice but to call the heating guy.

Harold Smith was the first to answer the phone. When the tall, dark-haired, blue-eyed man walked through her door, Kelly's heart went to pitter-pattering, her knees turned to jelly, and giggles she hadn't heard since junior high spewed from her lips. The man didn't even have to cast a line; she was already hooked.

Cam nudged her shoulder, breaking her reverie. "How's it feel to be so old, grandma?"

Kelly glanced at her seventeen-year-old, Zoey, and her fifteen-year-old, Brittany. "I think I've got a few years before anyone will be calling me that."

Zoey rolled her eyes and peered out the front window. Brittany shifted in her chair, crossing her leg. "Really, Uncle Cam, I don't even have a boyfriend. Don't even want a boyfriend. They're all too short for me anyway."

"There's gotta be some six-footers at the high school." Cam continued to tease her. "I bet Zoey could hook you up with one of her friends."

"Yuk. Zoey's friends are weird."

Malice slipped from Zoey's lips. "At least I have friends. I'm not some six-foot freak of nature that boys have to wear stilts to even come close to looking at eye-to-eye. I'm not—"

"That is enough." Frustration welled inside of Kelly. "We are not going to start—"

"Okay now." Kelly's mom clapped her hands then stood and grabbed Brittany's hand. "Why don't you show me that new soccer medal since your grandpa and I didn't get to go to your last tournament."

Kelly noted the pooling of tears in her middle daughter's eyes as she led her grandmother to the bedroom. Focusing her attention back on her oldest daughter, Kelly pinched her lips together. Zoey's body was tense and rigid. She stared at Kelly, as if to dare her mother to say something to her. *I don't even recognize this child, Lord. I expect some squabbling between the girls, but this hatred that Zoey seems to feel—I don't know what to do with her.*

"Time for cake," Harold hollered as he and Candy burst through the kitchen door.

"Grandma." Kelly heard Brittany's voice from the hall. "Come on. Cake."

Candy's eyes gleamed with excitement as the twosome walked toward Kelly with the pastry that seemed to be covered with entirely too much fire for a woman who still felt like she was in her midtwenties. "You'll love this cake, Mom." Candy's face flushed as she covered her mouth with her hand, as if trying to hold back a secret.

Kelly peered into Harold's mischievous gaze. There was no telling what he'd had the baker put on her cake—a tombstone, a cemetery. It had to be something pretty silly for Candy to get so tickled.

He lowered the cake in front of her. Kelly gasped. It was not what she expected at all. She drank in the bright red cursive icing that read, "WILL YOU MARRY ME?"

&

Harold watched as Kelly's deep blue eyes widened in surprise. She lifted one hand to her lips. He almost chuckled out loud at the outlandish sparkling mess of flowers or something that covered her hot pink fingernails. He'd always thought nail stuff was silly, and here he was. . .in love with a woman who was the queen of the gaudy stuff.

Harold nodded at Cam. Kelly's brother stood and took the cake from Harold's grasp. Harold lifted the half-carat marquise diamond ring from the icing and wiped off the band. Kneeling on one knee, he took Kelly's left hand in his. The light from the living room window seemed to cast a glow around her shoulder-length brown hair, making her look prettier than any angel he'd ever seen in pictures. This woman was entirely too girly, way too smart, too beautiful, too perfect for an old, get-your-hands-dirty, blue-collar guy like him. But the love that radiated from her tear-filled gaze nearly took his breath away, and he couldn't help but practically yell out a praise to the heavens. He swallowed and whispered, "I love you, Kelly."

She nodded her head ever so slightly. "I love you, too."

Her admission calmed his nerves, and Harold took a deep breath. Never in his forty years of existence did he think he'd be doing this. He was a hermit at heart, a huge fan of Oscar the Grouch on *Sesame Street*. Harold always connected with the green muppet's penchant to be a recluse, to do as he wanted, make a mess if he wanted, and to be left alone unless he wanted to make an appearance.

And as for women. . .as a boy, Harold might as well have been a card-holding member of the Little Rascals' Women Hater's Club. When he was a teen, he'd avoided the female species like grease avoids water. As a young man, he'd thrown himself into his work. Something about women—maybe it was that they cried for no reason, got all bent out of shape for no cause, or fussed over the most ridiculous things—made him want to stay away from the whole lot of the female population.

Or possibly it was that they whined over what their hair looked like and sprayed the poor mass with sticky stuff until the ends stood stiff and straight on the top of their heads. And why did they want war paint on their faces? If God had wanted their eyelids to be purple and green, he would have made them that way.

Sure, Harold had to admit they smelled awful good when a guy got home after a long day of working around sweaty guys and broken toilets or busted heaters. Still, did women really need all those bottles and cases he saw in the store to help them smell that way? It seemed a little ridiculous, if not quite a bit pricey.

Then he met Kelly.

The woman he'd driven to that local fingernail place more times than he could count over the last year. The woman who got her hair trimmed and colored more often than he did laundry. The woman whose war paint made her eyes sparkle and her mouth irresistible.

And everything changed.

Now he was willing not only to marry a girl, but take on three more of them. Teenagers and a preteen to boot. The irony of it welled up within him. *You have quite a sense of humor, Lord.*

He gazed back at the woman he longed to cherish for the rest of his life. He yearned to hold her, comfort her, protect her as only as husband could. Ever so gently, he caressed her knuckles with his thumb. "I've waited forty years for you. Will you be my wife?"

Without hesitation, she leaped out of her seat and wrapped her arms around his neck, making him lose his balance and fall to the floor on his back. Lifting herself off him, she sat up on her knees beside his body. "Sorry 'bout that."

A mischievous grin formed on her lips as he rose to a sitting position. He touched her cheek with the back of his hand. "I'm assuming that means yes."

She giggled, wrapped her arms around him, knocking him off balance again. His back hit the hard wood with a *thud*, but he hadn't felt a thing. Kelly Coyle was going to be his wife.

two

Kelly stuck the identification label she'd made for the new set of class novels on the inside flap of one of the books then handed it to Zoey to place on the bookshelf. "It's going to be kinda weird having your old mom for a teacher, huh?"

Zoey shrugged. She arranged a few books on the shelf, never turning toward Kelly.

Only seven years had passed since Kelly had finished her college degree. At the age of ten, Zoey's pride at her mom's accomplishment had been apparent. Despite having struggled in school, Zoey, from that point on, made every effort to earn good grades. Zoey had been successful, too. . .until Tim died. Since that time, Kelly's oldest child had spiraled more and more out of control.

Knowing that she had to keep trying, Kelly added, "I'm looking forward to having you in class. Language arts has always been your favorite subject, just as it is mine. We'll be able to share—"

"Do you really have to keep going with this song and dance?" Zoey peered at Kelly. Though they'd spent the better part of three hours working in Kelly's classroom preparing for the new school year to begin in only a few weeks, this was the first time today her daughter had so much as glanced at Kelly.

Kelly placed her hands on her hips, irritation welling in her gut. She'd spent the entire morning tiptoeing on pins and needles, searching for some way to connect with her oldest girl. "What is that supposed to mean?"

13

Zoey twirled her hand through the air. "This whole mother/daughter bonding stuff. I don't want to be here. You know I don't want to help you put your room together." Her tone dripped with sarcasm. "What? Are you hoping I'll tell you all my thoughts and feelings and that will make everything all better? That we'll be one, great big, happy family again." She spread out her arms, a snarl forming on her lips. "News flash, Kelly Coyle. Dad is dead. Things will never be all better."

"You will not take that tone with me." Kelly stomped toward her daughter. Though Zoey had grown a few inches taller than her mother, Kelly peered up at her child, demanding the respect she had not only earned, but as her mother innately deserved. "Every one of us lost your dad three years ago. We've all hurt—"

Zoey rolled her eyes then took a few steps back. "Yeah, some of us more than others."

"What is that supposed to mean?"

"It means"—Zoey grabbed her purse and walked toward the door—"I'm not going wedding dress shopping today. I'll catch you later."

"Zoey Coyle, you come back here." Kelly followed her daughter outside. Noting Zoey's car parked beside her own, Kelly cringed. She'd forgotten Zoey had met her at the school. "You're not leaving. You are grounded."

Zoey ignored her and kept walking. Before Kelly could reach her daughter, Zoey opened the car door, slid inside, and drove off. Kelly stared after her, the shock of her daughter's outright rebellion seeping through her skin. Zoey's defiance had hit an all-time high. Without a doubt, Zoey would be grounded. Kelly would take away the keys, the cell phone, the television, and whatever other privilege she could think of. But Zoey's problem wasn't one that could be fixed with punishment or discipline. Zoey's was a heart problem. *God she needs You so desperately, and I need to know how to be a good mom to her. Help me know what to do.*

❧

Harold gripped the cell phone tighter. "Do you want me to go search for her?"

Kelly's exhausted voice mingled with tears of despair. "No. She's going to be grounded when she gets home, but I'm going to wait until she gets there. I just needed to vent."

Harold bit back a reply. He didn't want to hurt Kelly's feelings, and he didn't want Rudy, who sat in the truck's cab beside him, to see his frustration at the child. From what he'd seen of Zoey, she didn't need the opportunity to do as she pleased until she got home. She needed to be disciplined— and now. If he had his say, the girl wouldn't be wearing black makeup and baggy black clothes. Her hair wouldn't be dyed black and tied up in knots all over the place. The child's appearance screamed she had problems.

Truth be told, Harold was a little embarrassed when they went places together as a soon-to-be family. He'd never tell Kelly that. He loved that woman with all his heart. And the other two girls, Brittany and Candy, well, they were as sweet and as normal as could be. Sure, the two younger girls fought and picked and cried and whined at each other over the slightest things, like which of them would sit in the front seat of the car or who had to do dishes which days, but they didn't look at their mother with contempt as Zoey did.

Harold sighed. He loved the teen. God had given him a paternal love for Kelly's girls that he would have never dreamed possible before he met Kelly; however, there were moments he found himself struggling to like Zoey.

Not that he hadn't tried to connect with his soon-to-be oldest daughter. He'd taken her to the movies, just him and her two sisters. He'd taken all three girls out to eat, played card games with the three and sometimes just Zoey. He'd picked her and her sisters up after school several times before she started driving. He even joined some group called "Facebook" on the Internet and tried to become her "friend." She denied his request. Nothing worked. She was cold, calculated, and downright disrespectful, and Harold had just about had it with her.

Now, he gets a call from Kelly, riddled with raw emotion, that Zoey had left the school in a huff and refused to go wedding dress shopping with her mother. The girl seemed to take pleasure in hurting Kelly. Harold cleared his throat. "I don't like it when she hurts you. Why don't I go find her?"

"No. Don't. I want this to be a good day. Brittany, Candy, and I will have a good time." She sniffed, and Harold knew she'd wiped her nose with a tissue. "You're still coming for lasagna, right? I'll have it ready by six."

"I wouldn't miss your lasagna for the world."

Her light chuckle sounded over the line. "I love you, Harold."

"I love you, Kelly. I'll see you tonight." He ended the call and slid his phone back into the case at his waist. Letting out a long sigh, he gripped the steering wheel.

"That girl's still giving her mom fits, huh?"

"Yep."

"Sorry to hear that. You know I raised two girls myself. It's not easy."

Harold looked at his most trusted worker. "How did you get through it?"

"I watched a lot of ball games and drank a lot of beer."

Rudy chuckled, and Harold simply stared out the windshield. Another reason he was glad he'd bit back any replies. Harold needed to be a witness to his friend. *God, help me live for You in the midst of this turmoil with Zoey. Help me be a good husband to Kelly, father to her daughters, and witness to those around me.*

The truth of his short prayer weighed on his heart. He would become the only living father Zoey would have from this point. He'd have to let God change his heart toward her.

❧

"I've been waiting all day for this." Fifteen-year-old Brittany slid into the front seat of Kelly's car.

"Who said you got to sit in front?" Candy stamped her foot and placed her hands on her hips.

"I got here first." Brittany stuck her tongue out at Candy.

"Mom, it's my turn!" Candy wailed.

Kelly raised her hand. "Enough." She pointed to the backseat. "Candy, you sit in the back. You can sit in the front on the way home."

"But—"

"No buts."

"Fine," Candy groaned as she slid into the back. "Where's Zoey?"

Kelly forced a smile. She refused to let the younger girls' squabble and Zoey's earlier actions take the joy out of the shopping trip. "Not coming."

"Oh no. What happened?" Candy growled from the backseat.

Kelly turned around in her seat. "Zoey doesn't want to come, and you know what, Candy, we're not going to worry about it." She looked at her middle daughter. "I pray for Zoey and her pain every day, but for now, the three of us are going to have a good time."

Brittany buckled her seat belt. "Finally."

"Where are we going to eat?" Candy asked.

Kelly smiled. Her youngest thought of little else but from where she'd receive her next meal. "Let's go to the boutique first."

Brittany let out a long breath. She twisted her purse strap between her fingers. "I can hardly wait to get there. I've been looking up dresses on the Internet this morning. There's just so much to choose from."

Not only was Brittany the most interested in sports, she was also a hopeless romantic. During the summer months, her sisters had to beg Brittany to stop watching one bride show after another. Candy, the dance queen of the family, knew the lyrics of nearly every song and the words of every movie she'd ever watched, but she was not overly interested in romance—which Kelly decided was a good thing since the girl was only eleven.

Kelly pulled into a parking space in front of the boutique Sadie, her sister-in-law, had suggested. The place was not at all what Kelly had envisioned, simply a small, office-style space in a strip mall of sorts. The store's name was posted in small, anything-but-ostentatious letters above the door. If Sadie hadn't suggested the place, Kelly would never have given it a second look. Kelly shifted the car into park.

"This is where we're going?" Brittany wrinkled her nose and pointed toward the plain door with such small lettering Kelly had no idea if it fronted a boutique or not.

"I guess so. Let's not judge a book by its cover."

Kelly and the girls stepped out of the car then walked into the boutique. Three hundred sixty-degree mirrors filled the back wall. Two ornately draped fitting rooms bookended each side of the mirrors. Rich paint and wallpaper covered the remaining walls, but Kelly couldn't help noticing the almost bare racks.

Candy tugged her arm. "I'm not so sure about—"

"Can I help you, ladies?" A man—who had to have only moments before hopped off a Harley-Davidson motorcycle— stepped out from one of the fitting rooms. His long, wiry, sandy-brown hair was tied back in a ponytail. His beard, a much redder color, was also tied in a ponytail at the base of his chin. His skin bore a coarse texture from years in the sun or acne or the combination of both. His black T-shirt and black pants had seen better days, but the black leather vest he wore appeared to be in good shape.

"Mom." Candy grabbed Kelly's hand, and Kelly felt Brittany take a step back.

Kelly lifted her chin. The man looked rough, but that didn't mean he was a bad guy. She didn't want her girls to prejudge the man, just as she didn't want to judge the shop. *Just as I don't want people to think I'm a bad mom when they see Zoey.* The inward admission pained her. Daily, she teetered between feeling like a failure and inwardly defending herself as a mother. Shaking the thoughts away, she smiled at the man. "I was looking for a boutique. I'm trying to find a wedding dress. . ."

"Yeah. I bought this place a couple months back. The man said he was losing money, but I've sure had a lot of women trying to buy dresses." He waved his hand around the room. "What you see is what's left. It's all half off."

"Maybe we should just go," Brittany whispered.

Kelly turned toward her daughter and smiled. "Half off? Honey, I think we're going to look around." Extending her hand, she took a few steps toward the motorcycle guy. "I'm Kelly Coyle. Nice to meet you."

He grinned and shook her hand. He looked past her. "Jim Lucas. Nice to meet you. Are these your kids?"

"Yes. This is my second wedding. Their father died three years ago. . . ."

"Sorry to hear that. My wife died about five years ago from cancer. If it hadn't been for the Lord. . ." He shook his head and took a deep breath.

"I understand completely." Kelly looked back at her girls, who had already begun to inch their way toward her.

Jim winked at the girls. "There's peppermint on the counter, if you want some. I'm going to keep working in the back. Let me know if you need anything."

Kelly turned toward her daughters. She shrugged. "See. You never know."

Candy cocked her eyebrow. "You don't exactly feel that way about Zoey's friends."

Kelly lifted her finger. "Ah, but you forget. I'm a high school teacher. I already know the kids Zoey hangs out with. We didn't know him."

"I guess that's true."

"Oh, Mom, look at this dress." Brittany's voice sounded from the other side of the room. "It's a Mon Cheri."

Kelly made her way over to her middle daughter. Her mouth dropped. "You're kidding?"

"Who's Mon Cherry?" asked Candy.

Kelly shrugged her shoulders. "I don't know, but I've got

to agree with Brittany. This dress is beautiful." She fiddled with the bodice of the gown. "Doesn't this thing have a size somewhere on it?"

Brittany pulled it off the rack and held it up to Kelly. "I don't know, but it looks close."

Excitement streamed through Kelly's veins. "Let's try it." She gently lifted the dress from Brittany's grasp and headed toward the empty fitting room. "Jim," she yelled, "is it okay if I use this fitting room?"

"Sure. Just ignore the mess." His voice sounded from somewhere in the back of the store. Kelly quickly took off her T-shirt and jean shorts then slipped into the dress. Thankfully, the dress zipped as well as having hook and eye buttons that covered the zipper. It was a tad big, but Kelly could hardly wait to see it in the 360-degree mirror.

She stepped outside of the fitting room. Both girls gasped. Candy covered her mouth with her hand. Kelly bit the inside of her lip and scrunched her nose. "Is that good? Is that a good gasp?"

"Turn around and look, Mom." Brittany turned Kelly toward the mirror.

Kelly closed her eyes. How would she feel seeing herself in a wedding gown? She had loved Tim completely when he was alive. Would seeing herself in this make her feel as if she'd somehow tainted his memory? She thought of Harold and how good and sweet he was to her and the girls. She knew Tim would have liked Harold. He would approve.

She opened her eyes and took in the straight, floor-length, ivory gown with off-the-shoulder lace sleeves. Delicate lace covered the soft silk material. The straight-line neck was adorned with dainty, floral, V-shaped beading. The same beading styled the waist and floor of the gown giving it a romantic and whimsical appearance. The gown was not too young looking, nor did it look like a dress to be worn by a mother. . .and Kelly didn't want to look like a mother on her wedding day, she wanted to look like a bride. Harold's bride.

"You look so pretty, Mom," Candy said.

"It's beautiful," Brittany agreed.

Tears pooled in Kelly's eyes. It was the first dress she'd tried on. "It's perfect. It couldn't be more perfect."

≈

Having just left the travel agency, Harold hopped into the cab of his truck and placed the Hawaii brochure and receipt on the front seat beside him. The honeymoon cost him a good deal more than he'd anticipated, but once Cam told him that Kelly had always dreamed of going to Hawaii, Harold knew he'd have to do whatever it took to get her there.

A slow smile bowed his lips. He and Cam had already discussed not telling Kelly where they would be going after the wedding. Cam's wife, Sadie, would pack her bags. His heartbeat sped up in anticipation. Harold could hardly wait to see the look on Kelly's face when she learned their destination. He latched his seat belt then glanced into his rearview mirror. "I've waited forty years for Kelly, surely I can make it another three months."

He turned the ignition and headed toward the shop. He'd left his right-hand man, Rudy, in charge of making sure the shop was clean and the trucks readied for the next day. It shouldn't have taken too long, as August tended to be a slower month in the heating, cooling, and plumbing business. It was the months that were the onset of hot or cold weather that usually had Harold and his men working more hours than the day possessed.

Which made a December wedding a bit nerve-racking for him. Oftentimes a good snow or two blanketed Delaware's countryside on or before Christmas, and Harold couldn't stand the thought of leaving his men one guy short while he was lying around on a beach in Hawaii.

"Don't think about it," he growled to himself as he parked the truck in front of the shop. "Cam promised to step in if it got bad while we're gone."

Harold got out and looked around the lot. Rudy's car was gone, a sign that the shop had been properly shut down and was ready for the next day. He made his way to the front door when a car pulled up the drive. He turned and smiled. Cam stepped out. "So, did you do it?"

Harold lifted the brochure and receipt in his right hand. "Got her right here."

"Let's see." Cam took the papers from Harold's grasp and fanned through them. "Man, Sadie will be so jealous. You know I'm going to have to plan a trip to the Islands now, don't you?"

"Sounds like that would break your heart?"

Cam grinned. "Not in the slightest." He rubbed his jaw. "But that's not why I'm here."

Harold folded his arms in front of his chest. "What's up?"

"Sadie's wanting the four of us to get together for dinner tomorrow night. She's already talked to Kelly."

Harold frowned. "That's all? What's the serious look for?"

"She wants to talk wedding colors and flowers and tuxes."

"Oh." Harold snarled. "I guess that goes with the territory."

Cam nodded. "Yep."

"And all I have to do is say yes to everything, right?"

"Yep."

Harold cocked one eyebrow. "You've gotten pretty good at this?"

"Yep."

Harold laughed out loud. "I'll be sure to heed your advice." He lifted the papers in the air. "I'm going to go lock these up and head over to Kelly's house. She's making lasagna."

Cam patted Harold's shoulder. "Have fun, my soon-to-be brother."

Harold chuckled as he made his way into his shop, stowed the papers in his wall vault, and went back to the truck. Cam proved to be a great perk to having fallen in love with Kelly. Not only did Harold find a woman he wanted to marry, but she came with a brother who'd become a good friend.

He glanced at the clock radio. Kelly was expecting him in half an hour. She'd gone dress shopping today, so Harold had already mentally prepared himself to listen to stories about lace and pearls and whatnot. He turned the ignition, noting his permanently stained fingernails, dry, calloused hands, and thick, hairy forearms. He was the beast marrying his beauty. What Beauty saw in him, he'd never know, but he sure thanked God for whatever it was.

Deciding he'd better stop for some gas, Harold pulled into an older, run-down gas station off Main Street. It was the usual hangout of some of the more shifty characters of their small town—a place he wouldn't want Kelly to frequent. But the owner was a man who God had laid on Harold's heart several years before, and Harold believed one day he would get Bill to come to church.

Harold finished pumping the gas then walked inside to pay. "Hey, Bill, how's it going?"

The balding, white-haired man hopped off the stool and

shimmied toward the counter. His weathered skin hung beneath his eyes and jaws. "Not too good." Bill's voice scratched from years of smoking. "Couple kids have been coming in and out all day. I'm pretty sure they're stealing stuff, but I ain't caught them yet."

"I'm sorry to hear that. Have you called the police?"

Bill shook his head and growled. "What am I gonna tell them? I ain't actually seen the kids. . ." He peered past Harold, out the store's window. "Here they come again."

Harold turned, and he felt as if his heart stopped in his chest. Zoey was walking toward the gas station. She was with a man whose shaggy hair stuck out beneath a well-worn cap. He wore dark clothes, even baggier than Zoey's, and Harold noted his several days' growth beard. More importantly, Harold noticed he appeared to be older, much older than any of the boys he'd seen in high school.

Without a second glance back to Bill, Harold marched out the door and straight to Zoey. Surprise registered on her face for an instant before she masked the expression with anger. "What's up, pop?" Zoey exaggerated the less-than-sentimental term of endearment.

"What are you doing here, Zoey?" Harold suppressed every ounce of fury that begged to be unleashed on the teenager.

"Getting a drink. Last I heard, that wasn't a crime."

Harold grabbed her arm. "I think you're going to go home with me now."

Zoey jerked away and scowled at him. "I will not."

"Hey, dude, what gives?" The man Zoey was with took a step toward Harold. "Zoey and I aren't doin' nothing wrong. You need to back off."

"I need to back off?" Fury raced through Harold's veins.

His fists clenched and he shoved them into his front pockets to keep from punching the young man in the face. "Do you know how old she is? Seventeen. That's right. This girl is still in high school."

The man smirked and crossed his arms in front of his chest. "Last I heard the age of consent was sixteen. She's plenty—"

Hot anger exploded inside Harold at the man's words. His fists came out of his pockets faster than he could control them. He grabbed the guy's grimy shirt in both fists, forcing his face mere inches from Harold's. "Now, you listen to me." The words spit from Harold's lips, splattering the man's face. "This seventeen-year-old is off limits for you, buddy. If I so much as see you within fifty feet of this girl, I'll. . ."

"Stop it, Harold." Zoey pushed his arm, but Harold was too enraged to move or respond. "I'll go with you. Just stop it."

Fear laced the young man's eyes, and Harold felt his anger start to simmer. The work of the Holy Spirit, no doubt. Twenty years before, Harold would have sent the guy to the hospital. Squinting his eyes, he held the man tight for just a moment more. "I mean what I said."

"Fine, Harold. You mean it. Let him go." Zoey pushed his arm again.

This time he released the young man and turned toward Zoey. "Go, get in the truck."

"My car is here. I'll just drive."

Harold shook his head. He didn't trust Zoey. She seemed to have mellowed from when he first approached them, and her tone had settled substantially, but he still didn't want to take the chance that she'd run off again. "No. Your mom and I will get your car later."

Zoey let out a long breath. "Fine." She turned toward the

man. "Jamie, give me my keys."

Shock coursed through Harold. "You let this guy have your keys? He's been driving your car?"

"You're mad. I get it." Zoey took the keys from Jamie's hands then started toward Harold's truck. "Can we just go home?"

Harold glared back at Jamie one last time. "I think you need to be heading on home now."

Jamie lifted his hands in surrender. "Fine. I'm gone." He turned and slithered back down the street.

Harold took several long breaths and rubbed the back of his neck with his hand. The age-of-consent comment Jamie made raced through Harold's mind repeatedly. What had Zoey been doing with that guy? Why was she so rebellious? Yes, she'd lost her father, but her family had been overwhelmingly supportive, and he'd tried, how he'd tried, to be good to her, her mother, and her sisters.

Before walking to the truck, he peered up at the clear, blue sky. The day couldn't be more beautiful—sun shining, slight breeze blowing. *Thank You, Lord, for stopping me before I pounded that boy. Give me wisdom with Zoey.*

Harold walked to his truck and slid into the cab. "Empty your pockets."

"Excuse me?"

Harold peered at Zoey. "You heard me. Empty your pockets."

Zoey's face turned scarlet as she pulled a few candy bars and a package of gum from her side pant pockets. Harold reached into his back pocket and pulled out his wallet. He pulled out a twenty-dollar bill. Grabbing her hand, he shoved it into her palm. She looked up at him and he locked onto her gaze. "I don't know how much you two stole, but you're going to take that candy and this money in there to Bill, and you're going to apologize. Hopefully, he won't press charges."

Shame wrapped Zoey's features, and for the first time, Harold witnessed a twinge of regret at what she'd done. A tear started to slip down her cheek, but she wiped it away in one swipe. "Fine. Give me just a minute, then you can take me home, pop."

The sarcasm and hatred were back, but Harold had seen a glimmer of hope. It twisted his heart in a way he hadn't expected. As much as she drove him to near insanity, the twist proved he cared for Zoey more than he realized. He wanted to see her straighten up, not just for her family, but for herself. *God, heal this little girl. Continue to work in my heart toward her, too.*

three

Kelly popped the last bite of cracker into her mouth. The first few weeks of a new school year always sent her stomach into a tailspin. She loved teaching, but the getting-to-know a new batch of teenagers, the settling into a routine, and the always-new requirements by the state and administration never failed to take a toll on her nerves. *It's why I'm able to stay a pretty good weight. One month of the year I live on crackers.* She chuckled to herself as she unlocked her classroom door, walked to her desk, and dropped her school tote and lunch bag on the floor beside the file cabinet.

Thankfully, it was Friday. She'd made it through the first three weeks of school, as well as having Zoey as a student, without a hitch. She noticed the three pictures of the bridesmaid dresses she'd narrowed her choice to sitting on top of a pile of ungraded essays on her desk. Adding planning her own wedding to everything else she needed to get done only enhanced her stomach's inner turmoil. She plopped into her rolling chair, making sure not to rest her elbow on the broken, left arm of the chair.

She picked up the three pictures. Her daughters would be her bridesmaids, or three maids of honor, as they chose to be called. Zoey didn't even want to go to the wedding, let alone be in it, but Kelly and her younger daughters deliberately ignored Zoey's pessimism and included the seventeen-year-old when they could.

Kelly clung to the slight change she'd noticed in Zoey after the night a few weeks before when Harold brought Zoey home for dinner. She never got a complete answer from Harold or Zoey about what happened that night, but she and Harold had gone to get Zoey's car at a gas station. Normally, Kelly would have demanded Zoey tell her what was going on, but something had changed in her daughter. It was small, almost unnoticeable, but it was enough that Kelly knew the Holy Spirit was instructing her to trust Harold.

She glanced at the pictures again. Two of them Brittany and Candy simply loved. The third dress her two younger girls didn't like, but it was the one Kelly knew Zoey would be most willing to wear. All of the dresses were practical, ones the girls could wear to church or to an occasion that called to be more dressed up. One of the dresses that Candy liked seemed just a bit old for her. It was appropriate for Brittany and Zoey, but. . .

Kelly cupped her hand over her mouth. "Oh my, why didn't I think of this before?" Favoring the right side, Kelly leaned back in her chair. "They're all in the same family of the deep emerald I'm using as my primary wedding color." She shook her head and laughed out loud. "And, they'd never be willing to wear the same dress after the wedding. I'll just have each girl wear a different dress all in the same color."

Still chuckling, Kelly turned toward her computer and booted it up. The students would be coming down the hall in five minutes or less. She clicked her e-mail to skim as many as she could before then. *To think I've been stressing over that for several days.*

She took a sip of her coffee, allowing the heavenly scent of hazelnut to wrap around her. It wasn't until after she started teaching seven years before that Kelly fell in love with the warm, caffeine-laden drink. Now, she couldn't start the day without it.

The first e-mail was from Harold. A smile bowed her lips. Each morning her man sent her an "I love you, and have a good day" e-mail. As she did every day, Kelly responded with the same message.

Before she could check any other messages, her students started to filter into the room. Extraordinarily tall and thin Logan Huff made his way through the door first, as he did every morning. "Hey, Ms. C."

"Hi, Logan. How has your morning been?"

"Good."

Logan made his way toward Kelly's desk. Most of the students congregated in the hall, spending every second they could with their friends before they were stuck in the classroom for over an hour. Not Logan. Instead, he spent his last few minutes talking with Kelly.

"I really enjoyed the reading last night," Logan went on. He pulled out a paper, and Kelly noticed Zoey walk in, place her books on her desk, and look toward Kelly and Logan. The boy continued, "I even made a few notes for our class discussion."

Zoey rolled her eyes then made a gagging motion. Kelly suppressed a smile. Zoey's action didn't contain the hatred it once had; it was done more in jest. Plus, Kelly loved to see that each day Zoey's makeup became a bit lighter and she wore a few actual colors of clothing on occasion.

The bell rang, and Kelly stood and walked around her desk. "I look forward to your comments, Logan. Now, go ahead and take your seat." She walked to the front of the room as the students made their way to their desks. "Good morning, everyone. Get out your warm-up sheets."

❧

Harold slid the keys out of the ignition, opened the truck

door, and slipped out. Excitement coursed through him as he made his way up the sidewalk toward Kelly's door. He'd been planning this Saturday excursion since before school started. Between starting back to school, the girls, and the wedding, Kelly had been stretched to the max. *This date will take things off her mind.* He smiled as the door opened before he had a chance to knock.

Kelly stood in the door, biting her bottom lip. "That smile looks quite mischievous. Should I be scared?"

Harold took in her long-sleeved T-shirt, jeans, and tennis shoes. Most of her hair was swept up in a ponytail, except the strands that weren't long enough, and her face appeared free of makeup. He whistled and winked at her. "You are adorable."

Kelly huffed, crossing her arms in front of her chest. "Are we going hiking? We better be doing something outside. You said to look natural, but if we end up at a nice restaurant, I'm gonna—"

Before she could finish, Harold wrapped his arms around her capturing her lips against his own. He could never get enough of the sweet scent of her perfume and softness of her lips. Pulling her closer to him, he deepened the kiss and she curled her fingers around his neck. The light scratch of her fingernails sent shivers racing down his spine, and Harold forced himself to pull away. "A little over two months until you're mine," he growled, then planted one last kiss on her forehead.

"That's too long," Kelly whined as her fingers traced a path through the back of his hair.

Harold took a step away from her and exhaled a long breath. "Woman, you are dangerous. Get your purse, and let's go."

Kelly giggled as she escaped back into the house, then reappeared seconds later with her purse strap over her shoulder. She shut the door and followed Harold to the car. "Can I get a hint?"

Harold opened the passenger's door for her then made his way to the driver's side. "Nope." He buckled his seat belt and started the truck. Kelly intently looked at her surroundings as Harold made his way toward Highway 1 South.

"How far are we driving?" Kelly quipped without looking his direction.

"It'll take us around an hour." Harold shook his head. The woman couldn't stand surprises. He assumed it was the teacher and the mother in her. She had to have everything planned to the last second, and she had to know what was going on.

"We're going to Dover, aren't we?"

Harold grabbed Kelly's hand, raised it to his lips, and kissed her knuckles. "I want you to sit back and enjoy our date."

"Okay. Okay."

Harold bit his bottom lip. He hated to say it, but he had to get Kelly's mind off their day's excursion. Mentally preparing himself for the onslaught of words, he planted a smile on his face. "Why don't you tell me where we are with the wedding plans?"

Kelly's face brightened. "Okay. Well, I picked out the dresses for the girls. I decided to let each wear a different. . ."

Harold listened as Kelly talked about dresses, ribbons, flowers, and other stuff he really didn't care much about. What he did enjoy was watching the happiness and excitement in Kelly's tone and expressions. He'd do whatever it took to make the woman he loved happy.

"You and the guys will need to get fitted for your tuxes in the next couple weeks."

Tuxes? He'd forgotten all about the fact that he'd have to wear a monkey suit. There had been only a select few times in his life that he'd worn a sports jacket and tie, never a full-blown tux. He was a jeans and T-shirt kind of guy, and the idea of someone taking a tape measure to him seemed weird. "You're going to go with us, right?"

Kelly clicked her tongue. "Nope. You, Cam, and your work buddies are going to go by yourselves. I don't want to see what you're wearing until our wedding day. Just make sure you don't get pink."

Horror smashed Harold in the gut. "They come in pink!"

Kelly laughed. "I'm kidding. Just pick black and white."

"Black and white, I can do that. I think." Harold turned toward his destination. Anticipation gurgled within him. He couldn't wait to see Kelly's expression. "It's just up ahead."

Kelly peered through the windshield. Harold peeked and noticed her eyebrows furrowed into a line. "I don't see a hiking trail or anything like that."

"I never said we were going hiking." He pointed toward the mammoth structure in front of them.

"The Dover International Speedway?" Kelly looked at Harold. "We've been together a year, and I never knew you liked to watch NASCAR."

Harold shrugged his shoulders. "I don't watch NASCAR."

Her frown deepened. "But?"

Harold grinned. "We're not watching. We're driving."

✌

Overwhelmed, Kelly followed Harold toward the Dover International Speedway, known as the "Monster Mile." She'd never been to a racetrack before and as they approached the main entrance the humongous monster statue mesmerized her. "Wow." She peered at the structure. The monster was a huge, gray, stonelike creature that burst through the top of a circular structure containing plaques of two hundred Dover Speedway winners. With his left hand gripping the top of the structure, the monster's right hand held a red and white racecar high into the air.

"It's something else, isn't it?" Harold pointed at its face. "His red eyes glow at night, making him even more fierce looking."

Kelly giggled. "His teeth kinda remind me of the abominable snowman in *Rudolph*."

Harold laughed. "Yeah. I can see that, but I don't think that's what they were going for." He grabbed her hand then pointed at the car in the monster's grip. "Come on. I can't wait to take a spin in one of those babies."

Kelly experienced a rush of stimulation overload. The place was huge, holding well over 100,000 spectators and the track itself was a mile long. Everywhere she turned she saw massive metal and concrete structuring and fences that seemed forever tall around the track. The bright-colored signs displaying various products were splattered all over the walls. Not to mention all the men and women clad in red shirts or a blue bodysuit of sorts.

While Harold took care of getting them set up, Kelly drank in the families who were taking pictures beside and inside the various cars. A person had to be eighteen to drive, but there were still plenty of young boys and girls rooting on their older siblings, parents, and even some grandparents.

Before Kelly knew it, she and Harold were in a "special van orientation" driving around the racetrack. She listened intently and thrilled when the time came for her final instructions with an in-car driving counselor. She was about to "ride and meet the Monster."

"So, do you think you'll like it?" Harold asked as he slipped one foot into the protective suit.

"Truthfully"—Kelly picked up her silver helmet with the yellow and red MONSTER RACING logo on the front—"I can't remember the last time I've had such an adrenaline rush. I can't wait."

Harold grabbed her close and planted a quick but firm kiss on her lips. "That's what I wanted to hear."

Kelly peered up at her man. The blue bodysuit mixed with the late morning sun gave his oceanlike eyes a brilliant glow. She touched his clean-shaven face. "You know, I've snagged myself quite a good-looking man."

"You don't look so bad yourself, Ms. Coyle, in that protective body gear. In fact, I'd say you look pretty enough to kiss again."

Kelly smiled as she allowed him one more kiss. Within moments, she slipped into the car. She rode as a passenger for four laps, studying how the instructor drove the vehicle as well as the course. Soon it was her turn to drive herself.

Trepidation raced through her as she considered driving the mammoth track in a speeding car. . .all by herself. She looked at her driving instructor. "How many laps do I drive by myself?"

"Ten."

Kelly's heart thrummed in time with the engines. "Okay."

"You're going to do fine. Remember, you don't have to go super fast. Just go at a pace you feel comfortable."

Kelly looked at the bright yellow stockcar that in only a

matter of minutes she would be driving. When had she ever had an opportunity like this? To essentially let her hair down and let the wind rush over her. She'd always been a planner, a detail kind of girl. Not spontaneous. Not a daredevil. And yet her adrenaline pumped at the idea of throwing away her inhibitions and driving as fast as she could around this track. Determined to conquer her queasiness, Kelly nodded at the man. "It's going to be great."

She maneuvered her way through the window and into the driver's seat. Tubing covered nearly every crevice of the inside of the car. She couldn't imagine how someone as big as Harold would fit into one of these cars; she felt like a sardine being shoved into its tiny tin.

When it was time, she started the engine and followed the instructor's car out onto the track. Harold drove behind her in a three-car "follow the leader" formation. The car rattled so hard, which the instructor had promised was normal, that Kelly felt her insides would be tossed into wrong positions. *It's a good thing I ate a light breakfast.*

The first lap around was not too fast but more thrilling than Kelly expected. She followed the instructor without a hitch and even enjoyed the jolt to a higher speed as they started the second lap. The whiz of her own car and the changing of the gears sent tingles of excitement through her, and Kelly found herself focusing on nothing more than the joy of the ride.

Too soon her trip was over, and Kelly found herself scooting out of the car's window. "How was it?" asked one of the workers.

"A blast!" Kelly pulled the helmet off her head and fluffed her fingers through her hair.

"That was awesome!" Harold approached her from behind.

Kelly turned. He'd already taken off his helmet and unzipped his suit. "I was hot as a July day in Bermuda, but that was so cool."

Kelly giggled at Harold's animation. He reminded her of one of her high school students instead of a forty-year-old business owner, but she understood his enthusiasm completely. "I agree. We need to do this again."

"You mean it." Harold raised his eyebrows in surprise. "I wasn't sure what you would think. Did you know we got up to ninety miles per hour?"

Kelly nodded. "I don't think I've ever driven over seventy-five."

Harold stripped off his suit then wiped small beads of sweat from his brow. "I don't know about you, but I'm starving."

"I think my insides remained intact." Kelly slipped her arms through the suit. "I think I could handle grabbing a bite to eat."

"All right, let's turn this stuff in and hit the road."

Kelly enjoyed the animation dancing in Harold's eyes. Tim had been a wonderful husband and father, but he'd never surprised her as Harold had. Tim would have never even considered taking his always-have-to-have-a-plan-and-be-safe-about-it wife to go NASCAR driving. Harold brought out the spontaneity in her. He brought out a need for adventure, and he wanted to have fun with her. She loved that about Harold.

God, You've been too good to me. You've given me a man who wants me to try new things, who wants me to have fun with him. Thank You, Lord. Help me to hand my cares over to You.

Harold returned and grabbed her hand in his. "You want to walk over to The Deli? It's just a little sandwich place that's right here at the speedway."

"Sounds good to me." Kelly squeezed his hand then leaned closer to him. "Thanks for this. I would have never guessed. . ."

"Well, I wasn't sure what you'd think, but I bet it took your mind off school, Zoey, and the wedding for a little while."

"Definitely." Kelly took a deep breath. "It was nice not to think about anything, to just have fun with you."

"Just being near you is fun to me."

Kelly thought of the three girls at home, probably this very moment arguing over who could watch which show and at what time. "You have no idea how fun your life is getting ready to be."

Harold stopped and turned Kelly to face him. "I don't deny it. You're a handful."

Kelly gasped and frowned.

Harold touched her cheek. "Let me finish. I knew when I started dating you that you came with three girls in tow. It was almost like God was playing a trick on me."

"Now wait a min—"

Harold put his finger over her lips. "But I love you. I love Zoey. I love Brittany. I love Candy. Somehow all four of you have wrapped me around your little fingers. And they're going to stress us out, but we're still going to have fun together."

Kelly kissed the tip of Harold's finger. "I love you, Harold."

"I love you, too." With her hand firm within his, he started walking toward the deli. "Besides, things will settle down after the wedding. You'll see."

four

"I feel like someone has shoved me into a shoe box and shut the lid." Harold shrugged then tried to lift his arms above his shoulders.

"No. It fits nicely." The saleslady adjusted the collar of the tux. "I suggest this vest to set you apart from your groomsmen in an ever-so-subtle way."

Harold looked at the piece of white material. It just looked like something else he'd have to squeeze his frame into, but it didn't matter to him. He just wanted everything to look nice for Kelly.

After slipping off the jacket, he put on the vest, buttoned it, then put the jacket back on. He looked in the mirror. He had to admit once he had a haircut and a good shave, the getup would look nice.

Turning toward Cam and his work buddies, Rudy and Walt, he stretched out his arms. "Well, guys, what do you think?"

"Not too shabby." Cam buttoned the second button on his jacket. "It's just a shame you don't look as good as me."

"Or me." Rudy wiggled his eyebrows as he sucked in his oversized stomach.

"No, I've got you all beat." Walt hefted the three-inches-too-short pants higher onto his stick-thin waist.

Guffaws sounded from all four men.

"Don't worry." The saleswoman smiled. "Everything will fit perfectly when you come back to pick up your tuxes. I think you all look handsome."

"All right then. Let's get out of these monkey suits and head over to Cam's for the big game," Harold said as he started to unbutton the vest.

"Now that sounds good," Walt said as he walked back into the fitting room.

"You can't get me out of this thing fast enough," Rudy added.

Once he'd dressed back into his comfortable blue jeans and T-shirt, Harold handed the items back to the saleswoman. "I'll take care of the paperwork if you all want to head on over to Cam's."

"Okay, see you there."

Harold watched as Cam, Rudy, and Walt walked out of the shop. The past several years Harold had been praying for Rudy's and Walt's salvation. Since Harold started dating Kelly, Cam had joined Harold in that prayer, and Harold had noted a softening in his workers, especially Rudy. Having decided weeks before that he would foot the bill for the guys' tuxes, he paid for the rentals then headed out the door.

He needed gas, and it had been awhile since he'd paid Bill a visit. In fact, he hadn't been back to the gas station since he'd encountered Zoey there two months ago. He knew he should have talked with Bill, and he probably should have been checking to make sure Zoey wasn't still frequenting the place, but one thing after another had kept Harold from being able to get over there.

"Well, now's as good a time as any." He hopped into his truck. He needed to pick up a few bags of chips, maybe a two-liter or two to take to Cam's house anyway. The guys had made it a regular Monday night event to watch that week's football game on Cam's wide-screen TV. Cam's wife and daughter would spend the evening at Kelly's doing one thing or another for the wedding.

Harold pulled into Bill's gas station. He pumped his gas then went inside. Bill sat behind the counter, coffee in one hand and the local newspaper in the other. Harold scooped up two bags of chips and a soft drink. "Hey, Bill. How's it going?"

A smile formed on Bill's wrinkled face, exposing the large gap between his front teeth. "How ya been, Harold? I haven't seen you in a while."

Harold nodded. "Yeah. I've been busy." Harold scratched his jaw, trying to think of the best way to ask about Zoey.

"Ain't seen that girl in here, either," Bill added as he totaled Harold's purchases.

Harold let out a breath as relief filled him. "I was going to ask you about that. So, she hasn't been around?"

Bill clicked his tongue. "Now, I didn't say she hadn't been around. Just not here." He placed the chips in a plastic bag. "I've seen her car driving up and down the street."

Harold's heart sank. "I was hoping—"

"She's still hanging around with some no-good characters, too."

"Thanks for telling me, Bill." Harold pulled out his wallet to pay, when he remembered he had a few business cards. He pulled one out and handed it to Bill. "Will you do me a favor?"

"Sure."

"The next time you see Zoey's car, will you give me a call?"

"I sure will." Bill shoved the card into his right front pocket. "Kids these days. Always up to no good."

"She sure has had me on my knees in prayer, that's for sure."

Bill huffed and swatted the air. "Like that will do any good."

Harold grabbed his bags. "It does me good. See ya later, Bill."

Harold made his way back to the truck. Bill was another one that Harold had been praying for years over. Now, he had the man keeping an eye out for his soon-to-be, wayward, Christian daughter. *Lord, what am I getting myself into?*

❧

Thanksgiving had finally arrived. The holiday felt especially sweet this year, and Kelly looked forward to Christmas and the few days after Christmas with such anticipation she could hardly contain herself. Kelly stopped cutting up slices of celery and wiped her hands on a towel. She opened the kitchen drawer she'd cleaned out and renamed "the wedding plans" drawer, pulled out a clear bag, and handed it to her mother. "This is the ribbon I've decided to go with for the bouquets."

"This is beautiful."

As her mother touched the soft fabric, Kelly's heart warmed with overwhelming thankfulness for her family and fiancé. She felt undeservedly blessed. "I'm glad you and Dad could come to Delaware for Thanksgiving. I can hardly wait to go dress shopping for you tomorrow."

Her mom shook her head. "I cannot believe I let you talk me into going to the mall on Black Friday."

"We'll have fun and you know it."

Her mom winked. "You'll have to go easy on me." She pointed toward the manila folder in the wedding drawer. "What's in that?"

Kelly handed it to her mom. "Pictures of the girls' dresses. Remember, I e-mailed them to you."

Her mother nodded. "Yes. They were very pretty."

Zoey walked into the kitchen. "So, are you going to finish the potato salad or talk about the wedding all day? Some of us are hungry, you know."

Noting the shocked expression on her mother's face, Kelly bit back her desire to yell at her daughter for such disrespect. Instead, Kelly forced a smile and grabbed several cans from the cabinet. "Why don't you help your grandmother and me? You make the green bean casserole."

Zoey snarled. "I don't know how."

"Why, Zoey Coyle," Kelly's mom responded. "You loved making the green bean casserole. Your daddy always said you made it the best of all of us."

"Well, he's not here now, is he?" Zoey retorted. She wrapped her arms in front of her chest.

Kelly's heart broke that her daughter still hurt so deeply over Tim's death, and she empathized with the teen's pain. But Zoey needed to stop making everyone else's lives miserable. Kelly shoved the cans into Zoey's folded arms. "Make the casserole."

Zoey glared at Kelly. "I don't remember how."

"Follow the directions on the fried onion can. It tells exactly how to do it." She turned and grabbed a glass pan from the cabinet. "We'll cook it in this."

"Fine." Zoey walked to the table and placed the ingredients on top of it.

The three finished Thanksgiving dinner in near silence. Occasionally, her mother would try to talk about school or their Thanksgiving menu, but Zoey would only mumble her replies.

"We're here." Kelly's sister-in-law's voice echoed through the house.

"Grandma! Grandpa!" Ellie, her young niece ran through the living room and into the kitchen. She spied Kelly's mom and wrapped her arms around her. "Grandma! I missed you."

"I missed you, too, sweetie."

While Kelly's mom bent down to hug the young girl, her dad walked through the doorway from the den. "Did I hear a little munchkin calling my name?"

"Grandpa!" Ellie squealed. She raced over to him and he picked her up. She pushed out her bottom jaw and pulled down her bottom lip. "Look, I lost a tooth."

"Well, you did," Kelly's dad responded.

"She sure did, Dad," Cam walked through the kitchen, stopping long enough to deposit a couple of pies and give Kelly and Zoey a kiss on the forehead and his mom a hug. "Head on back into the den so she can tell you how she did it. You've got the game on, right?"

Sadie rolled her eyes at Cam's words, and Kelly noted how the arrival of her brother and his family had lightened the mood of her home. She gave her sister-in-law a big hug. "I'm so glad you're here."

"I bet. I brought two homemade pumpkin pies." She placed the pies on the counter beside the ones Cam had deposited. "And a homemade pecan pie and a sugar crème pie. I've never made the sugar crème from scratch, so I guess we'll find out soon enough if I did all right."

"I'd be glad you're here even if you didn't bring food." Kelly glanced over at Zoey, who was arranging fruit on a tray and hadn't even uttered a greeting to her uncle and family.

Sadie winked and mouthed, "Got it." She walked over to the table and sat in the chair beside Zoey. "How's it going, Zoey?"

Zoey shrugged. "All right, I guess. Mom's making me help."

"At seventeen, I'm surprised she doesn't have you cooking the whole thing."

Zoey smiled. Kelly awed at the way Sadie could soften Zoey. From everything Kelly could see, Sadie didn't say anything special or specific that would make Zoey respond so positively to her, and yet she did. Maybe it was because there was just a little under a decade between their ages. More than likely, it was simply Sadie's attitude. The woman never judged Zoey—no matter what she wore, no matter what she said. There were times Kelly wanted to wring her oldest daughter's neck, but Sadie's belief remained steadfast that Zoey would be all right.

"Grandma!" Ellie called from the den. "Come here and see the cheer Candy and I made up for the ball game."

Her mother handed the wooden spoon she'd been using to stir the gravy to Kelly. "Here you go." She wiped her hands on a towel. "Okay. I'm coming, sweetie."

Kelly turned down the heat on the gravy. "Harold had better hurry. The food is almost done."

"Are you kidding me? Harold is coming?" Zoey asked.

Anger welled in Kelly. "Of course, he's coming—"

"He's part of the family," Sadie interrupted Kelly. She placed her hand on Zoey's. "I really like Harold. He's been good to your mom."

Kelly took several deep breaths as Zoey sat back in her chair. "Fine."

The doorbell rang and Kelly went to open the door for Harold. She hoped Zoey would be nice for the holiday. Her daughter had shown moments of an improved attitude, but with the holidays approaching, Zoey seemed to have sunk back into her shell. Kelly opened the door. "Hey, handsome."

"And there's my beautiful, soon-to-be wife." Harold wrapped his arms around Kelly and kissed her softly on the lips.

She closed her eyes and allowed his warmth to soothe her. Any hint of frustration slipped out of her mind at the tenderness of his touch. He released her, and she opened her eyes. "I needed that."

Mischief shadowed his gaze. "Well, you need never ask. I'm always available."

She smiled as she led him into the den. "Harold's here."

As her family greeted him, Kelly set the table that was meant to seat eight, but they were going to squeeze in ten. *A problem I'm thankful to have.*

With so many at the table, Kelly decided to leave part of the food on the counter and place the dishes she felt sure the family would eat seconds of on the table. Once everyone had filled their plates to overflowing, Kelly's dad said grace and the group began to eat.

Several conversations filled the room at one time and Kelly nearly burst into tears of thanksgiving yet again. They had so much to be thankful to God for. Her parents were healthy. Just a little over a year before, Cam and Sadie had married and were wonderful parents to Ellie. Her daughters were healthy, and God had given her the most wonderful man in the world to love for the rest of her life. Tears pooled in her eyes and she wiped them away with her napkin.

"This green bean casserole is awesome," Harold said. He took another bite. "I'm not usually a green bean fan, but this stuff is good. Who made it?"

Zoey jumped out of her seat. She slammed her napkin on to the table. "Is that a joke?" She peered Kelly. "Did you tell him to say that?" She looked back at Harold. "You are not my father!" She stomped down the hall and slammed of her door.

"What did I say?" Harold looked around the table, and Kelly felt an overwhelming sadness for the man she loved. He didn't deserve all the problems he'd be getting when he married Kelly.

"I'm sorry, Harold." Kelly shook her head as the tears pooled in her eyes anew. She could hear Cam explaining that Tim had always complimented Zoey's green bean casserole, but Kelly couldn't take anymore. She excused herself and walked into the bathroom. If she loved Harold, she wouldn't force him to endure all this.

☙

Harold sat on the couch in the den watching the Thanksgiving football game. Cam and his dad took turns rooting on their team and jeering at the referees. He could hear the girls in the living room playing board games. Normally, he would sit back and enjoy the game, but to his knowledge, Zoey still hadn't come out of her room.

He knew Kelly checked on her. Sadie went back there and talked with her for a long while as well, but the teen still hadn't rejoined the family.

Part of him wanted to tell her to stop all this nonsense and enjoy time with the family, that he would be a good stepfather to her. The other part of him understood her completely. It was the part that remembered being fifteen when his dad brought home the woman who would replace his mom who'd died only a few months before. *For years, I struggled with accepting that woman. But she was so patient with me.* Harold had lost both of them within months of each other only five years ago. *It's funny how I miss her every bit as much as I miss Dad.*

Cam's growl at the ref snapped Harold out of his reverie. He took a long swig of his soft drink. Just sitting there, not really watching the game, but worrying over Zoey was getting the best of him. He pushed up from the couch. "Be back in a sec, guys."

Kelly's dad just kinda shooed him out, and Cam didn't even look up. Harold walked through the kitchen and down the hall toward Zoey's room. He hesitated a moment. What would he say to her? *I'll figure it out if she lets me come in.*

He knocked, expecting her to growl or yell for him to go away. Instead, a small voice answered. "Come on in."

He opened the door. Her eyebrows rose in surprise when she glanced up at him. Just as quickly, she looked down at the small pillow that sat in her lap. She picked at the fringe. In the year that he'd dated Kelly, almost every time he'd talked with Zoey she had a hard edge, an anger that aged her well past her seventeen years. Today, she looked like a wounded twelve-year-old girl, one who'd lost her greatest treasure and could never get it back. He knew at that instant the only thing he needed to do was show her that he'd be there for her.

"What do you want?" Her tone expressed no emotion, simply asked the question with no anger, no frustration, no hope.

Harold shrugged. "Can I sit there?" He pointed to the chair in front of her desk.

"Sure."

Being sure to leave the door wide open, Harold pulled the chair away from the desk and toward the door. The last thing he wanted to do was to make Zoey feel uncomfortable. He sat, leaning forward to rest his elbows on his knees. "I'm sorry, Zoey."

She shrugged one shoulder. "Mom and Sadie said you

didn't know."

"I didn't."

"It was just—that was what Dad used to say. He'd go on and on about how good I made the green bean casserole, that I mixed it just long enough and cooked it at just the right temperature and for just the right amount of time."

Zoey paused, and Harold held his breath. She was talking to him, and he needed to listen.

"It was silly, really," she went on. "I knew he was exaggerating. Even as a little girl, I knew that. But I loved the attention. I loved that my dad was so proud of something I'd done."

She looked at Harold, brushing tears from her eyes. "You don't look anything like my dad, Harold. You don't act anything like him, either. Dad was a pencil pusher. He made good money working behind a desk. He was shorter and thinner than you and GQ good-looking."

Harold swallowed. He'd seen many pictures of Kelly's first husband. The man was a good-looking guy, and he did make three times the income Harold ever would. Just by looking at his picture, Harold could tell the man didn't mind being the center of attention. Harold tended to shy away from all that.

"I don't want another dad, Harold."

"I know that."

"But you want to be my dad?"

"Actually, yes I do."

"Why?"

Harold looked around the room, taking in the nearly all dark colors, fabrics, artwork, and furniture. Only a few light-colored things remained—the pillow she held in her hand, a family picture with their father in a white frame on the dresser, and a pink lamp that she'd probably had since she was born. "I guess because I love your mom and every part of your mom, including you and your sisters."

He leaned back in the chair, praying for God to give him the right words. "Did you know my mom died when I was fifteen?"

"Yeah. You mentioned it."

"Did you know my dad married my stepmom seven months later?"

Zoey scrunched her nose. "That is not cool."

"At the time, no, it was definitely not cool. But after I gave her some time, I found that she was a good mom. She couldn't replace my biological mom. Not really. But she was a good substitute. And I grew to love her. I want to be your, Brittany, and Candy's substitute. And I hope you'll grow to love me as well."

Zoey didn't say anything, and Harold knew that he didn't need to say anything else. He sat there for a little while, watching Zoey play with the fringe on her pillow. He didn't know what she was thinking, but her expression didn't appear hostile. He assumed she was trying to decide what to do with all that had happened in her life.

Finally, she looked up and pursed her lips in a half smile. "Thanks for telling me all that. I'll think about it."

Harold stood and put the chair back under her desk. "You want to come on out and join the family?"

"I will. I just need a minute more. You can leave the door open."

"Okay." Harold walked back into the den. Cam and his dad were so engrossed in the game he knew they didn't even know he'd left. *God, keep drawing that girl back to Yourself. Help me know how to be a good substitute.*

five

Kelly laid her newly pressed slacks on the edge of the bed. She grabbed the sapphire V-neck sweater off the back of the wingback chair that sat adjacent to the dresser. Her gaze took in the Victorian décor of her bedroom, all mauves and sages, aged lace and porcelain. This room was her favorite in the whole house.

It was her sanctuary—the place where God restored her soul during her quiet times of prayer, Bible reading, and meditation. After a long day she could walk into this room and feel almost instant relaxation. God had held her through many a worry and fear in this room.

In only two weeks, she would share it with Harold.

How she longed for the day that Harold could hold her in his arms. The day they professed their promise to one another as man and wife before their family, friends, and their Lord. The amazing beauty of it all was that her wonderful fiancé had actually mentioned he couldn't wait to join her in this room—and that he didn't want her to change a thing.

Lord, how could he have known that I love this room as it is?

Harold had been so good. He was always good. Steady. Faithful. Reliable. Everything she needed in a husband. Everything the girls needed in a father figure, even if Zoey didn't realize it yet. Even after her daughter's temper tantrum at Thanksgiving, Harold loved Kelly. And he loved the girls. Each one of them.

Releasing a long sigh, Kelly walked into the adjoining

bathroom with her sweater draped over her arm. Before she put the sweater over her head, she caught a glimpse of her reflection in the mirror.

At thirty-eight and the mother of three children, her body was definitely not that of a young woman. Normally, she paid little mind to the imperfections—but with the wedding only weeks away, insecurities she thought she'd put long behind her seemed to creep their way into her mind. Though not overweight, wrinkles, crinkles, and stretch marks had fashioned their way through Kelly's physique, and she cringed at the sight of them.

"Oh dear Lord, I want to be pleasing in Harold's sight."

A scripture that one of the older women from her Sunday school class said surfaced in her mind. Kelly had heard the verses many times before, but never in the context of marriage. Her wise friend knew Kelly would endure a time of uncertainty regarding her body. For that reason, Kelly had promised to tuck the verses away in her heart.

"Do you not know that your body is a temple of the Holy Spirit, who is in you, whom you have received from God? You are not your own; you were bought at a price. Therefore honor God with your body." She quoted the verses aloud.

Thinking about the verses in terms of marital intimacy seemed funny to Kelly. She'd quoted the verses many times to her daughters to encourage them to remain pure before marriage, but Kelly's seasoned friend's words were right. Once wedded, her body would be still be God's temple, but as a married woman.

Yes, Lord. Thank You, Jesus. Harold will be pleased with me, because my body is Your temple, and You've chosen us for each other.

Kelly slipped on the sweater then stepped into her pants. Within moments, she'd accessorized with a long silver chain necklace and matching earrings. She added a few spritzes of Harold's favorite perfume and stepped into her slight-heeled black shoes. She glanced at her reflection again. This time she smiled. "Not too shabby, future Mrs. Smith."

She glanced at her alarm clock. Harold should be there any moment. This was their last official date before the wedding. Harold was taking her to dinner and a movie; then they would stop by the mall to pick up a couple of Christmas presents.

The doorbell rang, and Kelly made her way to the door. The younger girls had gone to Cam and Sadie's house for the evening, and Zoey was working at her new part-time, fast-food job. She opened the door and before she could say hello, Harold had wrapped her into his arms and planted his lips on hers.

"You look beautiful tonight," Harold mumbled against her lips.

Kelly giggled and she gently pushed him away. "You haven't even had a chance to look at me."

His gaze never left her eyes. "I don't have to look at what you're wearing to know you look beautiful."

Her heart skipped a beat as she threw herself back into his arms. "Harold, I love you."

His fingers found their way to the base of her neck then up through her hair as he pressed his lips against hers again.

Kelly pushed away again and sucked in a long breath. She turned and grabbed her purse off the table and pushed him out of the doorway. "We've got to get out of here."

Harold furrowed his eyebrows. "Why?"

Kelly took long strides down the sidewalk and toward his truck. "Because the girls aren't home."

Realization etched across his face. "Yes, we do."

Kelly waited while he opened the passenger door for her. She slipped in then watched his large frame cross in front of the truck then into the seat beside her.

"This is going to be the longest two weeks of my life," Harold growled as he turned the ignition.

Kelly felt his frustration to her core. "Tell me about it." She picked at a piece of lint on her slacks, begging her mind to drift to something besides their wedding. In only a matter of moments, they'd left their small town and were heading toward Wilmington. "So, where are we going tonight?"

"It's a bit of a surprise." Harold placed his hand on her knee. "Would you mind if we didn't go see a movie tonight?"

Kelly felt a smile bowing her lips. She lifted her hand to one of her silver earrings and twisted it around her fingertips. "We're not going racecar driving, are we? I'm way overdressed for that."

Harold laughed and tapped the top of the steering wheel. "No racecar driving tonight."

Kelly lifted her eyebrows. "Are you sure? I'm willing to go home and change."

Harold laughed again. He peeked at her for just a moment, and the merriment in his eyes sent Kelly's nerves into a spiraling gyro. How she loved this man! "We had a lot of fun, didn't we?"

Kelly moved as close to him as she could without unbuckling her seat belt. "The best."

"Tonight won't be quite the adrenaline rush."

Mischief rippled through Kelly and she raised one eyebrow. "Just being with you is an adrenaline rush."

Harold howled. "That's right. But tonight, no movie. Okay?" He leaned over and kissed her forehead.

Kelly smiled, relishing the smell of his cologne on his neck. "That's fine with me. I love your surprises."

"It's settled then." He turned toward the mall. "We're going to pick up those last couple of presents you needed to get, then we'll head to dinner."

Kelly shrugged. "Okay." She opened her purse to find her lipstick and Zoey's cell phone fell out. "Ugh!" Kelly growled. "She stuck this in my purse at the store because she was wearing sweatpants. She must have forgotten. . ." She turned her body toward Harold. "I have no way to get in touch with her."

"Do you want to run it by her work?"

Kelly bit the inside of her lip. "Well, she works until eleven tonight, and you've planned the evening. When's the best time to take it to her?"

A Cheshire-cat smile formed on Harold's lips. "Since we're already in Wilmington, we'll wait until we've finished our date to take it to her. I can have you over there by nine o'clock."

Kelly looked at her watch. It was four. She figured dinner and a movie would have had her home a bit later. She had no idea what Harold had planned, but she knew she would love it.

❧

Harold touched the small of Kelly's back as they followed the guy, maître d', or whatever the fancy host person was called. Cam had told Harold the Hotel Dupont would knock Kelly out of her socks if she could stay there on her wedding night. So, before they headed out for Hawaii, they would spend their wedding night in this hotel.

He would have been just as content in a cardboard box on his wedding night, as long as Kelly was with him. But he'd learned one pretty big lesson in the year he'd dated Kelly—and her three daughters. Women were very different than men.

Kelly gasped as they walked into the dining room. *Wow. The place sure was something.* His soon-to-be brother-in-law wasn't lying. The most fancy, dark red curtains he'd ever seen hung over humongous windows. The room was paneled in thick, dark oak wood. Large chandeliers twinkled from the ceiling with matching chandelier-looking lighting between each window on the walls. The tables and chairs were the snazziest he'd ever seen with soft white tablecloths and cloth napkins and fancy flowers and lamps on the tables. Musicians played a light tune in the background. It was a bit overwhelming for a simple, plumbing-and-heating guy, but he had to admit the historical feel of it nearly knocked him out of the shiny, black dress shoes he'd bought for the wedding.

He sneaked a peek at Kelly. Her expression of complete awe and thrill filled his chest with happiness that he'd chosen to bring her here. Standing in this hotel, he may feel like a square pipe being shoved into a circular hole, but he'd be just fine if Kelly had a good time.

He pulled out her chair, and Kelly slid into it. "Harold, this is amazing." She touched the tip of one of the fancy-folded napkins. "I've always wanted to come here."

Harold sat in the chair across from her. He looked at the array of glasses and silverware and whatever else was sitting in front of him and realized he had no idea how he was supposed to eat at this place. He looked up and into Kelly's sparkling eyes. "Cam told me you would love this place."

"I do." Kelly traced her finger around the top of one of the glasses. "But do you have to pay to stay at the hotel to eat here? Probably not. I'm sure they set up reservations, don't they?" Kelly furrowed her eyebrows. "This has to be awfully expensive. Harold, you do too much. You're too—"

Harold lifted his hand to stop her. "Kelly, I'm forty years old. I own my own business, and I've been a bachelor all my life. I can afford this, and it was part of a. . ."

He hesitated. He'd planned to wait until dessert to tell her this was where they'd spend their first night as man and wife. He'd hoped to watch her have a wonderful meal and then surprise her about the plans. She still didn't know they would be going to Hawaii for their honeymoon, and he planned to keep it that way.

The worry that etched her brow urged him to share his plan early. "We're going to spend our wedding night here."

Kelly gasped again. This time her eyebrows lifted in surprise, and she covered her mouth with her hand. Harold noticed the tips of her fingernails were a bright red and she had candy canes painted on both of her ring fingernails. He almost chuckled aloud at the irony of the scruffy plumber with the dolled-up teacher.

He grabbed the hand that covered her mouth. Lifting her knuckles to his lips, he kissed them gently. "Since we'll be at our reception the night of the wedding and then we'll be leaving for our flight in the early afternoon the day after the wedding, we won't be able to enjoy one of the Dupont's famous dinners on the night we stay here. I didn't want to take that treat away from you, so I arranged for us to share our Hotel Dupont dinner today."

Kelly leaned closer to Harold. Her free hand reached up and touched the side of his jaw. Harold's skin seemed to burn at her touch, even more so as their wedding drew nearer. "You are so good, Harold Smith, so, so good. How I praise God for you."

Harold smiled at her compliment. It was he, the old, scruffy, nowhere-near-as-educated bachelor who felt humbled and awed that she would accept him.

Before he could respond, a waiter dressed in a getup that may have cost more than the coat and tie Harold was wearing approached their table. He and Kelly opted for soft drinks, and Harold tried to focus as the man rattled on about goat cheese and mushroom cappuccino and other things he'd never heard of that they would choose from to be their first plate. Harold tried to appear interested and able to understand what the guy was saying, but who had ever heard of mushroom cappuccino? It sounded gross.

His frustration must have been apparent as Kelly smiled at him when the man had finished. "Honey, if you'll try the chicken broth, medley of vegetables and chicken meatballs, I'll try the field greens and tomato carpaccio, and cantaloupe-peppercorn emulsion and maybe we can taste a bit of each other's."

Harold wasn't sure he understood what Kelly was getting, but he knew the words chicken and meatballs were for him, and that sounded good enough. He looked up at the waiter. "I think she has a good plan."

"Wonderful."

Harold reached over to take Kelly's hand in his, but the man began to prattle on about second dishes. Oh boy. Again, Harold tried to figure out what the guy was talking about, but all he could do was focus on the small mole on the guy's neck. It was in the shape of a star. He'd never seen a mole look like that.

Kelly saved him again, ordering some fancy shrimp for his second dish. When the man went on to the third plate,

Harold wondered how long this would take. But this time, he heard the words "black Angus" and Harold knew what that meant. A good steak. Now, the guy was talking Harold's language. What red-blooded American man didn't love a good steak?

The guy finally left and Harold leaned toward Kelly. "You know I have no idea what I'm eating—except the steak."

Kelly giggled. She took the napkin from the center of the plate and placed it gently in her lap. "You know I would have been just as happy at a regular old steakhouse, as long as you were with me."

Harold smiled at the sweet woman beside him. "I know. But I also know that you love that we're here right now. I want to make you happy. Next time we'll go to that regular old steakhouse."

"Deal."

❧

Kelly leaned back in the passenger seat. She enjoyed the dancing of the city's lights as Harold drove out of Wilmington and toward their hometown. The hotel dinner had been absolutely marvelous. The waiter was wonderful, the ambiance stunning. It had been a treat she'd remember forever. She peeked at her fiancé who silently studied the road. *God, You have been too good to me.*

Her cell phone vibrated in her purse. She glanced at the clock. Sadie would have dropped the younger girls off at the house around a half hour before. Kelly was surprised she hadn't received a phone call with them fussing before this. She pushed the talk button.

"Mom, Candy won't let me watch my show. She had the TV last. Now it's my turn," Brittany squealed.

Kelly sighed. No "Hi, Mom. How was your date?" Just instant fighting. She could hear Candy's voice in the background. "Mom, it's that law show. I hate that show. It scares me."

"You watch it all the time in Mom's room. You just don't want to watch it right now," Brittany retorted.

"Brittany." Kelly tried to get her middle daughter's attention. "Brittany." She tried a little louder.

Harold looked at her and grinned. Kelly rolled her eyes. "Brittany."

"Mom, tell her," Brittany squealed.

"Brittany, I'm not going to let either of you watch TV if you don't listen. Let me talk to Candy."

"Mom wants to talk to you." Brittany's voice sounded muffled, but Kelly could still make out the mocking in her tone.

"Mom," Candy whined into the phone.

"Listen, you can go in my room and watch TV."

"I don't want to sit in that old, stuffy wingback chair," Candy whined.

"Just cuddle up in my covers." Kelly brushed a hair from her face. "I'll be home in just a bit."

"Really." Excitement sounded in Candy's voice. "I get to get in Mommy's bed." Candy's voice singsonged at Brittany, then the phone clicked off.

No good-byes. No "Did you have fun, Mom?" Just squabbles. It was the story of her life.

Harold laughed, and Kelly scowled at him. "Just you wait, Mr. Smith. You get to listen to this all the time, too, in just a few weeks."

"I'll be hiding out in my man room."

Kelly chuckled at the room in her house that Harold had started to fix up as his man room. He hadn't brought his leather recliner and TV over because he hadn't moved out of his house yet, but she knew they would be finding a home in her house only a few days, or maybe hours, after they returned from their honeymoon.

As she put her cell phone away, she remembered Zoey's. "Don't forget we have to take this to Zoey." She pulled out her daughter's phone and accidentally pushed the middle button turning it on. Curiosity crept through Kelly as she noticed her daughter had a new text message. It was from a boy, but Kelly didn't recognize the name.

"Would it be bad to check your daughter's text messages?" She looked at Harold sheepishly.

"I don't think so."

"I was just being silly asking. Of course I'll check her messages. It's my job as her mom to make sure she stays safe."

Kelly opened the text and read it. Her mouth fell open and her blood seemed to stop flowing. "Oh no."

"What?"

Kelly could hear the worry in Harold's tone, but she couldn't look at him. Her eyes couldn't seem to leave the phone's screen. "Oh no."

"What is it, Kelly?" Harold tried to reach for the phone, but Kelly held it tight.

"Get me to that fast-food joint. We've got to get there fast."

She looked at the time again. According to the message, Harold had about fifteen minutes to get to the hamburger place before Zoey left.

"What is it?" Harold's voice pleaded again.

Kelly looked at her fiancé. Worry etched his expression, and she hated that this wonderful man was being dragged through all the difficulties she was having trying to raise her children.

"Tell me, Kelly."

She tried to hold her tears back. Harold hadn't had the blessing of holding the girls as babies, of getting slobbery kisses on the cheek, of seeing them reach huge milestones like using the potty and reciting the ABC's. Instead he met her when they're at the stage of arguing, complaining, being selfish, and making poor choices. *God, how can I do this to him? Sure, there are rewards with the girls at this stage of life, but it seems to be more about saying no, explaining why I say no, and ending sibling fights.*

"This isn't fair to you, Harold. I'm like walking chaos." She turned her body toward him and placed her hand on her chest. "And I don't like drama. I've never liked drama, but now I live with drama every day. Some days I think I've gone cuckoo from the overwhelming surge of girl-drama that happens throughout the course of one of my days."

Her humor fell flat as she inwardly acknowledged her selfishness at being willing to involve Harold in her life. Dating him had been wonderful, but the closer they got to marriage, the more she realized she was asking too much of him.

She thought of the Christian counseling sessions they'd had. At their small community church, the pastor required six sessions of counseling for all engaged couples before he'd wed them before God and family. Her and Harold's sessions had been especially sweet to her because she had been able to hear how Harold felt about taking on a ready-made family of all girls.

"*I don't know a lot about women.*" Harold's words just a few weeks ago filled Kelly's mind. "*But I know I love this woman.*" He'd pointed to Kelly. "*And all the Coyle women.*" His smile and quick wink had warmed her heart. "*I don't know what it's like to be a biological father, but when I see one of Kelly's girls get hurt, I know I want to help them. When I see them smile over something they're proud of, I feel prouder. When I see a boy looking at them inappropriately, I want to punch him in the face.*"

The last statement brought a smile to her face even now. *In the last year, he had proven his love for them. But now with Zoey . . .* Her thought broke and she closed her eyes. What was her oldest child thinking? *God, what will it take to bring her back to a right standing with You? How can I help her?*

She'd tried everything every Christian counselor had ever suggested. The girl simply refused to allow herself to heal from her father's death. She wanted to blame God. And the child was old enough—seventeen and a senior in high school—that all Kelly could do was watch the girl's emotional upheaval.

But this I can do something about. Kelly gripped Zoey's cell phone tighter.

"Kelly, tell me what's going on." Harold's voice broke her thoughts.

"She's meeting a guy after work."

Harold nodded. "Okay. That's not so bad."

"No." Kelly shook her head. "The boy's intentions for that meeting are written in the text. And she told me she was getting off at eleven, but she's supposed to meet him at nine thirty."

Anger etched on Harold's features as his foot pressed more firmly against the gas pedal. By all accounts, he looked like a father on a mission to save his little girl. The picture warmed Kelly's heart but saddened her, as well. She knew Harold loved the girls, even though Zoey especially was at her most difficult. His life had been much simpler before Kelly came along.

The guilt of it weighed her, and then she thought of the confrontation she and Zoey would no doubt have in just a matter of minutes. She felt older. Tired.

She didn't feel like a two-week-away bride. Nor like a woman who had just spent a romantic dinner at one of the nicest places she'd ever been to.

She felt like an old, weary woman, who was in for yet another "battle of her life." *God, I feel like I'm losing.*

six

It had been an uphill battle getting to this day, but they'd made it. Harold looked at the calendar on his cell phone. December 28. His wedding day. Battle or no battle, Kelly Coyle—soon-to-be Smith—was worth it.

Harold buttoned the last button on his white vest. The thing had some kind of pattern on it. He thought the woman had called it paisley. It made him nervous that Kelly hadn't gone with him to pick it out. He wanted this wedding to be all that Kelly dreamed. At least Cam had gone with him. Kelly's brother knew more about clothes than Harold did.

"You don't look half bad." His friend, Rudy, walked into the Sunday school room turned men's dressing room. Walt followed behind Rudy.

Harold grinned at his friends. The two had surprised him by attending the church's Christmas service. Walt had even brought his wife and children. They hadn't talked much about it since, but Harold knew it was a start. And he clung to God's promise that His Word never comes back void. No matter what, he'd continue to pray for his friends.

Rudy patted his round belly. "I think I look ten pounds thinner."

Normally, the pair reminded Harold of the villains from the movie *Home Alone*. Seeing them decked out in black tuxes made Harold smile. "I'd say that you two don't look too shabby."

"Maggie thinks I'm hot." Walt straightened his shoulders

then wiggled his eyebrows.

Harold and Rudy burst out in laughter. Harold nudged the taller man's shoulder. "It's good your wife thinks you look good."

Cam walked into the room. He clasped his hands together. "Are you ready for this, big brother?"

Harold felt excitement race through his veins. "Ready to be your big brother? You bet."

ঽ৶

Kelly looked at her daughters. The girls' green dresses fit beautifully and complemented the frame and personality of each one. Candy's deep green silk taffeta dress hinted at the eleven-year-old's budding shape but still allowed her to look like a girl. Brittany's knee-length silk spaghetti-strap dress accented her long, slender features in beauty and innocence. And Zoey—as much as Kelly didn't like the darker hair color, she couldn't help but admit the mixture of dark hair, light skin, and emerald green made the teenager look stunningly beautiful. The dress they'd chosen for Zoey was fashionable, but still hid the curves of her oldest daughter.

Kelly shook her head. *It was only a few years ago that I didn't have to worry about their clothes revealing too much.* Her mind drifted to the night two weeks before when she and Harold had stopped Zoey from meeting a boy at his house. Kelly purposefully shook the thought away. Today was her wedding day. She wanted to focus on Harold, and the life they'd share together.

"I have a present for each of you." Kelly pulled three small boxes from her bag.

Candy clapped. "Oh, I can't wait. I love presents."

Brittany moved closer, eyeing the boxes, but Zoey stayed

across the room from them. Kelly knew she wasn't thrilled with the wedding, but her oldest had been moping since Christmas Eve, and Kelly wished she'd snap out of it, just for today at least.

"Each of you is wearing a beautiful dress, individual, as if made especially for you." Kelly smiled at her girls. She and Tim had made beautiful children, and each of them held such wonderful, unique qualities to place at God's feet for service. "But I wanted you to have one thing that's the same. I hope you like them."

She handed boxes to Candy and Brittany, then walked over to Zoey and handed the last one to her. At the same time, the girls opened their gifts. Kelly watched as Brittany allowed the slight gold chain to drape her fingertips. The small diamond pendant hung from the chain.

"It's so dainty," Brittany said.

"So pretty," Candy added.

"I'm afraid I'll break it." Brittany said. "You know how I am."

Kelly laughed. Yes, she knew her middle daughter. The girl would lose her head if it were not attached to her body, and she was just as fortunate her feet were attached as often as she tripped over them. "You'll be fine. Here, let me put it on you."

Amidst thank-yous from her younger girls, Kelly put the necklaces around Brittany's and then Candy's neck. She walked toward Zoey to help her with the necklace, but her oldest already had the necklace on. Kelly gazed at her daughters. They were so big, so grown up. The years had gone by too fast. After inhaling a deep breath, she glanced down at the sweatshirt and T-shirt and jeans she still wore. "Okay, one of you go get your grandma. We gotta get my dress on me. She was waiting for me to give you your presents before she came back in here."

Candy giggled. "I'll get her."

Kelly walked toward the garment bag protecting her wedding gown. She'd forced herself not to look at it for the past several weeks as she yearned for the day to arrive. She started to unzip the bag, but the zipper stuck. She zipped it back up just a bit to be sure the zipper was lined up right. She unzipped it again; this time a piece of the antique white fabric caught. Kelly gasped. "Oh no."

She tried to gently pull the fabric away from the zipper's teeth, but the metal seemed more determined to bite into her beautiful dress. Anxiety welled within her, and her hands started to shake. "No. No. No."

Tears pooled in her eyes as she tried not to tug on the zipper or the fabric too hard.

"Here, Mom, let me help." Zoey stood beside her. She nudged Kelly out of the way, then gently and quickly released her dress from captivity.

Kelly blew out a sigh of relief. "Thank you, Zo-bow." The nickname she'd called her oldest as a baby slipped from her lips. She grabbed her daughter in a quick hug.

"Mom, I need to talk to you."

Zoey's voice sounded urgent, but Kelly could only focus on pushing the plastic away from her dress. "Where's Brittany?"

"She's in the bathroom. I need to talk to you alone."

"Okay. Go ahead." With the dress now plastic-free, she allowed her fingers to trace the exquisite beading. She could hardly wait to get into this dress, for Harold to see her in it.

Kelly's mom walked through the door. "Let's get that dress on you. You're getting married in only half an hour."

Excited trepidation raced through her. Even though Kelly

felt moments of guilt at allowing Harold to take on her crew of crazy women—well, lately, it had been her trying oldest daughter—still, she could hardly wait to meet Harold in front of that pulpit and say "I do."

"I guess I'll talk to you later." Zoey's voice sounded small and for the first time in a long time, a bit unsure.

Concern inched into Kelly's gut, but she pushed it away. "We'll talk during the reception. I promise."

❧

Harold tried to inconspicuously hush his groaning stomach as he stood beside the pulpit, waiting for his bride. He had no second thoughts about marrying Kelly, but standing in front of a mass of people, half of whom he didn't know, in a monkey suit, made his knees quake.

He never realized their church was so big and could hold so many people.

The pastor leaned toward him. "You look like a man about to get married."

"That bad, huh?" Harold pulled the fancy napkin from his coat pocket and wiped the beading sweat from his forehead.

The pastor chuckled quietly. "Second thoughts?"

Harold grimaced. "No. I just don't feel comfortable in front of all these people."

Cam must have overheard, because he nudged Harold's elbow. "You're doing fine."

The music started, and the church doors opened wide. Harold calmed as the attention of the guests diverted to the back of the church.

Candy walked ever-so-slowly down the aisle. Her face beamed and she held her shoulders almost too far back. He didn't know for sure what paternal feelings felt like, but he believed he experienced them for Kelly's girls. Everything in him wanted to wrap that eleven-year-old in a bear hug and tell her what a pretty young lady she was becoming. He could see she wore the delicate necklace he and Kelly had picked out for each of the girls. Kelly wanted their gift to be special, and he agreed the small necklaces were perfect.

Brittany walked down the aisle next. So tall and slender, the teen was a combination of model and basketball player. With her hair all knotted up with shiny stuff and flowers and that dark green dress fitting her shape a little too snuggly, if someone asked him, Harold knew he was feeling some paternal feelings because his gaze instantly scanned the room to detect any young guy who might be checking her out.

Brittany reached Candy at the front of the church, and Harold winked at both of them. Their cheeks were flushed, and he knew they were happy that he and their mom were getting married. He looked forward, and Zoey stood at the doors. *If only she could be happy for her mom and me, as well.*

With everything in him, Harold believed one day he and Zoey would be friends. He didn't know if she'd ever allow him to be a true father figure, but if she did, he'd take the role seriously and do the best he could by her. He couldn't believe how lovely she looked walking down the aisle toward her sisters. Her dress was every bit as pretty as her sisters and her hair was just as fixed up, but sadness filled her eyes. Harold hated that.

But she didn't appear angry. Maybe that was a step up. Harold prayed she hadn't been hard on Kelly while they were getting ready. Taking in the sweet expressions on the younger girls' faces and the fact that all three of them were wearing the small diamond necklace, Harold believed their afternoon had gone well.

Only one more girl to walk down the aisle, and he would see his bride.

"Here comes my little munchkin," Cam whispered beside Harold.

His daughter, Ellie, wore a shiny white dress and held a small basket that was decorated with dark green ribbons and small red flowers. She dropped white and red rose petals on the white carpet. The girl looked like a smaller version of her mother, Cam's wife.

Ellie finally took her place beside Zoey, and the church doors were shut again. The music changed, and the congregation stood. Harold had to swallow the knot in his throat. He could hardly wait to see Kelly.

The doors opened again, and his bride stood in the doorway. Her father stood beside her with her arm tucked into his. Unbidden tears welled in Harold's eyes. *God, what have I ever done to be given such a beautiful woman?*

Her dress was stunning. The church's dimmed lights semmed to make it glitter. He couldn't see her face, as a veil covered it. How he longed to see her face!

What did a man want in a wife? A woman who encouraged him. A woman who respected him. A woman who made him feel like more of a man. And if she was as beautiful as Kelly on top of all that, well. . .

Emotion threatened to overcome him. He wasn't a crying man. He was simple. A forty-year-old bachelor. A heating guy, the plumber. He was happy working with his hands and living alone, until he met Kelly Coyle. Then everything changed.

Finally, she and her father reached the end of the aisle. It was time for her dad to pull back the veil and give Harold her hand. Her father kissed her cheek; then she looked at Harold. Her eyes glistened with love, and Harold wanted to scoop her up and head out of the church with her. He wiped his palm against his pants before he took her hand in his.

The pastor began to speak of love and commitment. He read scripture from 1 Corinthians about the meaning of love. "Love is patient, love is kind." The words had been etched in Harold's heart years before through Bible study and listening to his pastor. In the last year, Harold had lived those words, not just heard them, not just read them. Now he knew them. And nothing would change his love for Kelly. Nothing.

"Do you take this woman in sickness and in health, for better or for worse. . ." the pastor's voice continued on.

Harold squeezed Kelly's palms. This woman worried too much about the "for better or for worse" part. She worried over what the stress of having three girls would do to him. He'd have to spend the rest of his life proving to her how much he loved her and the girls. . .for better and for worse.

When the pastor had stopped talking and it was Harold's turn to speak, he squeezed her palms again. "I do," he answered with his mouth. His gaze urged her to believe he meant those two words to the core of his being. They were true, and they always would be.

಴

Kelly took in the reception hall decorated in dark green and deep red. She'd had the most beautiful Christmas wedding she'd ever seen. It wasn't overly expensive, nowhere near as ostentatious as a few weddings she'd been to over the years, but it was still the best she'd ever experienced.

Her girls seemed to be having a good time talking with one relative or church member or another. Many of her colleagues from work had come to support her day, and Kelly was exhausted and overwhelmed by the many people who'd attended. More than she'd expected.

"It's time to cut the cake," Sadie announced over a microphone.

What would Kelly have done without her amazing sister-in-law? The woman had taken care of every loose end in addition to being in charge of the reception food.

"I want cake, Aunt Kelly." Her niece Ellie pulled at the bottom of Kelly's dress.

"Okay. Let Uncle Harold and me cut it first, then we'll get you some."

She smiled and skirted away toward her dad.

"Uncle Harold?" Harold lifted his eyebrows.

"That's who you are now."

He grinned and leaned forward and kissed her lips softly. "I like it."

"No more kissing. We want some cake!" Cam hollered, and Kelly watched as Harold's neck turned a bright red.

She picked up the knife and had Harold wrap his hand around hers. They cut two small slices together. She squinted at him. "Are you going to be nice?"

"Yes. I want you happy later," he whispered.

This time Kelly felt her cheeks warm as he eased a bite of cake into her mouth and she smashed the piece in his. Howls of laughter filled the room.

He wiped the smeared icing from his jaw with his fingertips. "What was that for?"

She shrugged. "I guess I'm not worried about you being happy later."

Harold grinned and dotted her nose with some of the icing

on his finger. "No, you don't."

He moved closer to her. She tried to give him a mean look, but she knew laughter lit her eyes. "Harold."

"Okay." Sadie's voice halted his lunge at her. "Since the bride and groom have to be going, we're going to toss the bouquet and garter now, then eat cake afterward."

Kelly glanced at the clock at the back of the reception hall. It was getting late, and she didn't want to be tired for their trip, wherever they were going, tomorrow. All she knew was they had a long plane ride ahead of them. She looked at her sister-in-law and mouthed, "Thank you."

Sadie grinned and winked as she arranged the single girls in a spot on the floor. Each of Kelly's girls stood in the mix, though it was obvious Zoey was less than thrilled. She threw the bouquet and one of her fellow teachers caught it. Within moments, Harold had tossed the garter.

Harold grabbed her elbow. "Are you ready?"

Warm tingles shot through her at the look of longing in her new husband's eyes. "You bet."

"Mom, I need to talk to you."

Kelly broke eye contact with Harold and looked at the owner of the voice. "Zoey, I forgot. Harold, make sure everything is in the car."

"You know they've trashed it."

Kelly rolled her eyes. "I've seen it. Tell Rudy and Walt and that brother of mine that I said thanks."

Kelly turned back to Zoey. Her daughter's eyes were so sullen, so frightened. It was as if Kelly were looking at her more then a decade ago when her new puppy had died. Something was wrong with Zoey, and Kelly had been so wrapped up in the day she hadn't taken time to really listen.

In only moments, she'd be leaving, but she would listen now. "What is it, Zoey?"

Tears fell from Zoey's eyes. It was sudden, as if a dam had burst and now the waters couldn't stop. Fear wrapped Kelly's heart. Sobs wrenched her daughter, and Kelly guided her to the back of the building, away from anyone who could hear them.

"What is it, Zoey? Tell me."

"Oh, Momma."

Momma? Zoey hadn't called her Momma since long before Tim died. A vision of her wearing her favorite orange and pink pajamas and swinging on her swing set in the backyard slipped through Kelly's mind. "What is it, Zoey?"

"I can't tell you." Her words jumbled together and her nose started to run. "You'll be mad at me. I don't know what to do."

Kelly pulled up a chair and sat Zoey down in it. The girl didn't fight her, and Kelly grabbed another and sat across from her daughter. "I might be mad at you, but you have to tell me."

Fear and confusion welled in Kelly's heart. What could it be? Had she stolen something? Was she taking drugs? Was she failing school? Was she—

"Mom, I don't know how this happened." Zoey looked into Kelly's eyes. Her daughter's eyes were bloodshot and swollen from crying. "I was being so careful."

Kelly closed her eyes. *Oh no. Oh, no, no, no, no, no.* "Zoey, what do you mean you were being so careful? Are you—"

"Mom, I'm pregnant."

Kelly's world crashed around her. Her heart thudded inside her chest as she tried to process what her daughter had just said. Memories of past students who'd gotten pregnant in high school flooded her mind. Most didn't graduate. Their lives were difficult. They weren't ready.

Sleepless nights, soiled diapers, hours of colic raced through Kelly's mind. The constant worry the first few months that the baby would die while sleeping. The moments of indescribable frustration because the baby wouldn't stop crying. Kelly peered at her daughter. *Zoey is not ready for this.*

She looked down at her wedding dress. This was the end to her perfect day. In moments, she was supposed to get in a car with the man she loved and spend her first night with him as husband and wife. Then she was to get up and go on a honeymoon, spend a full week away from her children. And this was her parting news.

She looked at her daughter, broken and devastated. Pity and sorrow enveloped Kelly. *She has no idea how this will change her life. God, will this be enough? Will she finally surrender?* Kelly shook her head. *A baby? How would they handle a baby?*

Zoey's crying escalated. "I'm sorry, Mom. I told Jamie. He doesn't care. I haven't seen him since I told him. I don't even know where he is."

Kelly sucked in a deep breath. She didn't even know who Jamie was. Dreams of Zoey's wedding, of her future, seemed to evaporate before Kelly's eyes. Kelly wrapped her arms around her child. God would see them through this. He'd seen her through so much in her life. This wasn't too much for them. "It's okay, Zoey."

"I know you're mad at me."

Mad? No. Disappointed? Well, yes. Overcome with sorrow? Absolutely. I'm desperately hurt for her. So hurt.

As her own pain threatened to take over her body, Kelly held Zoey tighter. "I'm not mad at you. I'm sorry for you that you'll have to go through this so young. But I'm not mad at you. I love you, and God can work *all* things together for His good."

Believe what you just said, Kelly, she inwardly encouraged herself. Taking a deep breath, she begged God to fill her with a peace beyond her understanding. Her thoughts calmed, and she knew God would see them through this, just as He'd seen them through Tim's death.

Zoey snuffed, and Kelly marveled that her daughter hadn't thrown a fit at the mention of God. "I am sorry, Mom."

Kelly placed her hands against Zoey's cheeks. "Listen to me, child. We'll get through this. We just have to trust God, and that doesn't mean it will be easy."

Zoey nodded.

"I think we're all set." Harold's voice boomed down the hall.

Kelly's mind raced. She couldn't leave now. She needed to call a doctor, find out about this Jamie, make sure everything was all right. "Harold, I don't think—"

"Try to have a good time, Mom." Zoey hugged Kelly, and Kelly relished her daughter's touch. Zoey whispered, "Don't say anything right now. Go on your honeymoon."

Kelly touched Zoey's arm, keeping her voice loud enough for Zoey alone to hear. "I don't think I can go now."

"Yes, you can. You need to. I've been okay for two months."

"Two months?"

Tears brimmed Zoey's eyes. "I just couldn't tell you. I was so embarrassed."

Kelly exhaled a long breath. She studied her daughter, then looked back at Harold.

"Please go, Mom." Zoey nudged her toward the door.

Inwardly torn, she knew they would need this vacation, as

things would change drastically sooner than they'd all believe. Kelly nodded and looked back at Zoey. "It's going to be okay. Try not to worry." She kissed Zoey's forehead. "We'll talk when I get back."

Zoey nodded and left the room.

"Is everything all right?" Harold furrowed his brows.

She shook her head. She didn't want to do anything to make him worry during their trip. They'd have plenty to think about when they got home.

seven

Harold shoved the boogie board beneath his arm and walked farther out into the ocean. Hawaii was more beautiful than he would have ever imagined. He'd only been to the beaches in Delaware, but the water around this state was crystal clear. It reminded him of ice cubes, only hot. He didn't have the words to describe how pretty this place was.

He turned his head, peeking back at his bride of only five days. Kelly would have the words to describe this place—his wife, Mrs. Kelly Smith. He loved the thought of her being his wife. The past five days had been as close to heaven as he could ever imagine. The ocean. Kelly's soft dark hair. The palm trees. Kelly's soft skin. The warm air. Kelly's sweet whispers of love. He'd never been so happy.

With ocean water up to his waist, Harold turned and pushed the boogie board in front of him. The next good wave he could see coming, he'd jump, chest first, onto the board and ride in on the wave. Boogie boarding was nowhere near as strenuous as surfing, but for a guy who would probably never visit Hawaii again, unless it was for a second honeymoon with his bride, boogie boarding was good enough.

He looked back toward the beach. Kelly sat in a beach chair with a magazine in one hand and a water bottle in the other. She looked absolutely adorable in Brittany's oversized white sunglasses. Her middle daughter had left a note in the suitcase telling her mom she needed to look cool in Hawaii. The black-and-white polka dot bathing suit Sadie packed looked awfully good on her as well.

Harold waved at her, and Kelly dropped the magazine and waved back. The smile she graced him with was full and beautiful, and Harold knew he was blessed.

A good wave pushed him from behind, and Harold turned, noting another one coming. He jumped on to the boogie board, allowing the water to push his oversized frame forward toward the beach.

What a rush! He pushed off the board once the wave had died. Cradling the board beneath his arm, he walked toward Kelly and his lounge chair. He'd been boarding for a while and needed a break. At the very least, he needed a drink of water. When he reached Kelly, he realized she was on the cell phone. Again.

He dropped the board and fell into the chair. After opening the cooler, he grabbed a water bottle, opened it, and took a long drink. Kelly had spent a lot of time on the phone since they'd gotten to Hawaii. She'd spent a lot of time on the phone before and after their flight and even at the Hotel Dupont in Wilmington.

Maybe that's normal for a mom. He'd expected her to talk with the girls once, twice, maybe even three times per day while they were gone. He knew she would enjoy the time with him, but he knew she'd miss the girls, and they would miss her. But it seemed she talked to them more like ten times a day. Literally. Like every two hours.

Harold stuck the bottle back in the cooler and leaned back in the chair. He folded his hands behind his head and exhaled a deep breath. The funny thing was most of the time she was on the phone with Zoey. It seemed like all of a sudden, since Kelly left Delaware for ten days, Zoey needed her mother almost every minute.

Maybe that's a good thing. Maybe the teen will be ready to straighten up. Maybe she'll turn back to God. In Harold's experience with the teenager, he'd never witnessed her living for the Lord. Kelly and Cam often talked about Zoey's zeal for the Lord and telling her friends about Christ before her father's death. But that had been three years ago. All Harold had known was sullenness, darkness, and rebellion.

And yet, he cared deeply for the girl. It seemed an odd thing to him. He wondered when he first started dating Kelly how he would handle her kids. It wasn't as if he had his own kids to have given him some experience. He didn't even have any brothers or sisters. He'd had zilch experience with people under the age of adulthood, well, except the ones he ran into on heating, cooling, or plumbing jobs. Then he was often pulling toy cars and miniature doll heads out of the toilet.

But when he met Kelly and he saw that his feelings for her were growing serious, he hit the carpet, asking God to show him how to be a good male influence on those girls, to show him how to love them. It had been a true miracle, in his eyes anyway, because Harold did love them as if he'd been their father all along.

Kelly hung up the phone and put it in a bright yellow bag that was covered in big pink flowers. She sighed ever so slightly, but Harold still heard it. He studied his new wife. "How's everything at home?"

She smiled at him, the bright, beautiful smile that drew him each time she did it. "It's good."

But he knew something was wrong. Her eyes held just a hint of worry behind them. They had since they'd left the reception. Since he'd returned from checking on the car while she talked with Zoey. She'd assured him that Zoey's tears that day were just the same old stuff, but he had the nudging feeling that wasn't the complete truth.

"You know I haven't talked to the girls but once a day since we left. Do you mind if I call them?"

Kelly shrugged. "Sure." She pulled the phone out of her bag and handed it to him. "They'd probably like that."

Harold turned on the phone and noticed that almost every call to and from Kelly's cell was with Zoey's phone. He pushed the HOME number and Candy picked up the line.

"Hey, Squirt."

"Harold!" she squealed. "Have you gotten me a souvenir yet?"

Harold laughed. He knew that would be Candy's first thought. "We've gotten you one thing, but we're going to get you something else when we go shopping later."

"I get two things!" Candy yelled. "Brittany, I get two souvenirs from Hawaii." Her voice took on a bragging lilt, and Harold couldn't help but laugh out loud. Brittany and Candy fought over everything, and when Kelly reminded them they'd be friends one day and the girls vehemently denied it, Kelly would roll her eyes and say she was praying against them.

Brittany's voice suddenly sang over the line. "Hey, Harold. Are you having fun?"

Harold could hear Candy whining in the background at her grandmother that Brittany had stolen the phone from her. "Your mom and I are having a blast. Hawaii is gorgeous." He turned and winked at Kelly. "But nowhere near as pretty as your mom."

"Ew, gross, Harold."

The voice changed on the line again. This time it was Candy again. "What did you say? What's gross?"

Harold laughed. "You'll have to ask your sister. Is Zoey

there, too?"

"Yeah. Just a sec." Her voice muffled as she started yelling for Zoey.

A moment later Zoey's voice sounded over the line. "Hi, Harold."

"Hey. How's it going?"

"Fine."

Harold pinched his lips. Zoey sounded different. Less edgy. Less angry. Less confrontational. "So, what do you want from Hawaii?"

"You don't have to get me anything. I'm fine."

Kelly poked his arm and motioned for him to let her have the phone. "Well, your mom wants to talk with you. Tell the girls I said bye."

He handed the phone to Kelly. Part of him wanted to tell the girls he loved them, but it still felt funny to say it. Kelly had been the first woman he'd ever said the words to. He'd barely said them to his parents before they died. He just wasn't good with words and all that. He was a man of action. A man who showed the people he cared about how he felt through doing things for them.

But he'd also learned from Kelly that girls like to hear nice things, too. The girls' daddy had died. He was the only one they'd get to have here on earth. If they let him, he'd be the one to walk them down the aisle, to hand them over to a husband, as Kelly's dad had handed her over to him. He wanted to be a good father to them. *Lord, help me.*

Peace surrounded him. Now that he and Kelly were married, things would settle down. He'd have time to learn to be a good father figure. The girls were handfuls, but they were still young. Things would only get easier.

৯

How am I going to tell Harold about this? Kelly stared at her reflection in the mirror. She looked like a woman who'd spent the last several days sunning on the beach and enjoying time alone with her new husband. Her skin was sun-kissed, making her blue eyes sparkle along with the diamond stud earrings and diamond pendant necklace. The white sundress Sadie had packed for her was one of the prettiest Kelly had ever seen and complimented her shape in all the right places. Her sister-in-law was a fashion whiz, and Kelly determined she'd never again go shopping without her.

But looks can be deceiving. And she had no idea how Harold would respond when she told him the truth about Zoey. She, herself, still didn't know how to respond. It was true her daughter seemed broken, but Kelly couldn't tell if it was from repentance or from the fact that she got caught.

Kelly closed her eyes and gripped the edge of the sink with both hands. "Oh Jesus, I'm not ready for this." Kelly peered back at her reflection. "And Zoey really isn't ready."

She flopped onto the toilet seat cover. "And Harold isn't going to be ready." Leaning forward, she placed her elbows on her legs and rested her forehead in her hands. "I never should have married Harold. I was being so selfish."

Raising teenagers had proven to be the most difficult thing Kelly had ever experienced. When Tim died the challenges seemed to have tripled. She loved her girls, wouldn't change a moment with them. She wouldn't even change the different quirks that made each one a unique young lady. But life would be so much easier if all of them wanted to live their lives in obedience to God and to their mother.

"That would be a perfect world," she mumbled and then

chuckled at herself. "I wasn't the easiest teenager for my mom and dad to live through, either."

She sobered and exhaled a deep breath. "But I was the biological child of both my mother and father. I've married a wonderful man and forced him into the chaos I'm living in."

Her heart broke at the coarseness of her thoughts. When had she become such a negative thinker? When had she lost her faith in God, her trust that He would take care of everything in their lives?

God, I haven't lost my faith in You. You are my anchor, my core, but I feel so desperately guilty, so selfish for forcing Harold into all this. I'm not worth all the frustration and confusion and—she lifted her hands then smacked them down at her sides—*just everything.*

And a baby? What would they ever do with a baby? Zoey wouldn't be able to go to college; she'd have to get a job. And who would watch the baby? And what kind of job could she possibly get? The thought of diapers and bottles and formula and all the things a baby needed swirled through Kelly's mind. *Babies were expensive.* Zoey would be completely dependent on Kelly and Harold for financial help. The whole thing was overwhelming—and unfair to Harold.

She knew Harold loved her. It was evident in the gentleness of his touch, in the way he helped her in every aspect of her life—from the mundane of changing the air filter to providing a new outfit for Brittany's school dance. She couldn't question he cared for her and the girls.

But what will he think when I tell him?

She stood and shrugged at herself in the mirror. "He has to know."

"Know what?"

Kelly gasped when the bathroom door opened and Harold

stepped inside. Her hands started to tremble as tears pooled in her eyes.

He pointed to the floor. "I forgot my sandals in here."

Kelly's gaze traveled to his shoes then back to his eyes. She bit the inside of her lip as her hand found its way to the diamond stud earring. Twirling it around, Kelly's heartbeat raced.

"Tell me, Kelly. What's going on?"

"I'm sorry, Harold." She covered her face with her hands. "I'm so selfish."

He wrapped his arms around her, and Kelly felt safe in his embrace. Harold was strong, so strong, and she wanted to lean into him, allow him to be her strength through the time that lay ahead of her. But he shouldn't have to deal with a new baby. He was a forty-year-old man. He'd been a father for only five days. In less then nine months, he'd be a grandpa. The idea was absolutely preposterous.

He released his embrace, gripping her arms gently in his hands. "Tell me, Kelly. We're in this together."

Yes, they were in this together. If she'd loved her husband as much as she believed she did, she never would have dragged him into this. But he had to be told. Taking a deep breath, she peered into his eyes. "Zoey's pregnant."

❧

"Zoey's pregnant." Kelly's words from a few days before washed over him again. He leaned back against the airline seat. The announcement had put quite the damper on the rest of their honeymoon. They'd gone through the motions, lying on the beach, eating Hawaiian cuisine, and trying to enjoy their time together.

But the announcement had changed things. Kelly

emotionally pulled away from him. He didn't know how to explain it exactly, but he felt it in her gaze, in her touch, even in the way she talked to him.

She'd said that she was selfish, and he knew what she meant. They'd discussed it many times before during their premarital counseling and on several of their dates. She felt guilty dragging him into a house of crazy teenage women.

He didn't know how many times he'd told her that he loved them and that he wanted to be a part of their crazy house, but she simply wouldn't believe him. To him it was a matter of her not taking him at his word. And Harold lived by the integrity of his word. His business thrived because if he told someone he would do something, then he would do it. He didn't understand why Kelly didn't believe he meant what he said. He'd proved himself many times over to her.

And what would they do with a baby? He didn't think he'd even held one. Anytime he'd ever been around one it was screaming its head off.

He looked at Kelly in the seat beside him. Her head was tilted to one side, her mouth slightly open. She'd fallen asleep. He knew she was exhausted. She hadn't slept much since she told him.

She smelled like that purple lotion she was always putting on. He loved the smell of it. And she looked so cute, probably ten years younger than she was, with her just slightly burnt nose and cheeks. Everything in him wanted to take her hand in his, lift it to his lips, and kiss her knuckles. But he couldn't.

He looked forward, staring at the gray plastic tray attached to the back of the seat in front of him. He unlocked the tray and let it rest as a small table in front of him. He'd get a drink of ginger ale when the flight attendant came by. His stomach was a bit queasy. If he were honest with himself, he'd admit it wasn't from the plane ride, but from the fact the woman he loved didn't trust him.

eight

Nearly two weeks had passed since they'd returned from the honeymoon. Kelly had been overwhelmed with schoolwork. As one of the senior trip sponsors for the school, she'd been doubly overwhelmed planning the trip to South Carolina—the trip she'd hoped would bring her and Zoey together. Instead, Zoey wouldn't be going, and she and Zoey were together on some emotional level every night.

Jamie, the much older boyfriend that Kelly didn't know about, seemed to have left the state of Delaware. Though Zoey mourned about it all day, every day, Kelly couldn't help but be thankful the guy was gone. From the pictures she'd seen of him in Zoey's phone, the man did not appear to be the kind of son-in-law she hoped to have. *I know. I know. Appearances can be deceiving.* She inwardly scolded herself. *But I'm not sure I can take much more, and the guy has already proven to lack a good deal of integrity by getting his teenage girlfriend pregnant and then leaving the state.*

Kelly took a deep breath. The bitterness she felt for the man threatened to set in on a daily basis. She constantly took her feelings to the Lord and begged Him to help her feel His mercy.

"Are you ready, Mom?"

Kelly turned at the sound of her oldest daughter's voice. The child no longer wore the darkest makeup she could find. Her face was scrubbed clean and her hair pulled back in a ponytail instead of falling over her eyes. Her attire had changed dramatically, as well, and Kelly knew her oldest wasn't spending all her time with her old peers. Instead, she spent all her time with Kelly. Usually crying. Always moping.

"I sure am." Kelly forced herself to smile. Heading to the obstetrician for the first time, she and Zoey would learn how far along she was in the pregnancy and if everything appeared to be fine.

"I'll be in the car." Zoey walked out the door. Kelly grabbed her purse and followed behind her. Kelly had hoped the pregnancy would encourage Zoey to return back to God, and she had stopped "doing" the things she'd been doing before, but her heart was still hard. So hard. The truth of it wounded Kelly's spirit.

Visions of watching Zoey raise her grandchild in an ungodly environment plagued her thoughts. Watching her daughter slip into the front seat of the car, her expression sad and a bit sickly encouraged the worry to well in Kelly's heart.

"Trust in the Lord in all your ways and lean not on your own understanding." She paraphrased the proverb in her mind. She had to trust God in this. *Besides, after the appointment, we're going to tell the family tonight. All of them.*

The reminder that her entire family was coming for dinner that evening made her wrinkle her nose. She couldn't even imagine what everyone would think. Sadie would understand, as she'd experienced an unexpected pregnancy and gave up the baby for adoption. As circumstances would have it, years later Sadie married the adoptive father, Kelly's own brother Cam, almost two years after his wife died of cancer. *But what would the girls think? Candy and Brittany?*

She shook the thought away. *One thing at a time.* She pulled into the doctor's parking lot.

"Are they going to examine me?"

Kelly looked at Zoey. Fear wrapped her daughter's features. "Probably."

Zoey studied her hands. It reminded Kelly of Zoey's first day of kindergarten. It was Zoey's telltale sign of being nervous. Her oldest was just a child, and she was having a baby.

Kelly placed her hand on Zoey's. "It's going to be okay. I'll go in with you if you'd like."

To Kelly's surprise, Zoey nodded. "I can't do this alone, Mom."

Truer words had never been spoken, and it pained Kelly's heart that her daughter wouldn't have a loving husband by her side to go through the pregnancy and birth of this baby. She squeezed Zoey's hand. "I'll be here. But more importantly, God will be here. You're not alone."

Kelly expected her daughter to sigh or roll her eyes or make a smart-aleck comment at Kelly's mention of God. Instead, her daughter nodded, unbuckled her seat belt, and quietly slipped out of the car.

Hope welled in Kelly's heart. *Draw her back to You, Lord. Draw her back.*

❧

Harold had been in a sour mood all day. He'd snapped at Rudy for leaving a tool in the wrong spot when as it turned out Harold was the one who'd misplaced it. He'd apologized to his long-time employee, but he still felt miserable.

And he definitely didn't want to go home.

He passed by his old house. Technically, it was still his house. Having been a bachelor for so long, Harold had paid it off some ten years before. Kelly didn't owe anything on her, well their, house because she'd paid for it with an insurance settlement after Tim's death. The two of them didn't need money, so he'd leased his house to a young family in their church who needed it far more than he did.

They still paid him a little bit of rent, just enough to cover the insurance and taxes, and part of the agreement was they'd do the upkeep on the house. Harold noticed the shoveled sidewalk and driveway as well as some kind of wreath on the front door. It appeared they were doing as they promised.

Life had been so much simpler when he lived in that house. After a long day at work, he'd have gone home, changed out of his work clothes, heated up a TV dinner, and settled into his recliner for a night of basketball or football or whatever sport was playing.

Now he returned home to a most-of-the-time home-cooked meal, which beat out the TV dinner, but then on Mondays and Thursdays he took Candy to dance. On Tuesdays and Thursdays he also took Brittany to basketball conditioning practice, not to mention picking her up from regular basketball practice on Mondays, Tuesdays, Wednesdays, and Fridays. If Brittany had a game, everything changed, and if she had it the same night as church or Candy's dance practices, then it really threw everything off.

He had no idea how Kelly had done it as a single mother. He was the family chauffeur, and while he ran the girls to their various activities, Kelly did laundry, cooked dinner, cleaned the house, and all the other household activities that had to be done. The girls had chores, but they were often running so much they didn't have time to do them.

"Welcome to the life of the modern-day family," Kelly had said to him a week after they'd gotten married. She'd been teasing, and he loved spending time with the girls, but his life had taken a real turn after they returned from the honeymoon.

He turned onto their street, noting that Cam and Sadie had already arrived. He blew out a breath. Zoey's appointment had been today. If everything was fine, they were going to tell the girls and Cam's family tonight. Ugh, he dreaded this. He pulled into the driveway and took his keys from the ignition. *Might as well get this over with.*

He walked into the house and spied Kelly in the kitchen. She looked so pretty in her light blue sweater. It was one of his favorites. After making his way to her, he couldn't resist placing his thumb beneath her chin and lifting her face so he could give her a kiss. He released her and she smiled up at him, her expression one he remembered from a month ago—before Zoey's news had turned their world upside down.

"How did everything go?"

"Everything is fine." She lightly nodded her head, and he knew she was letting him know they'd be sharing the news tonight.

"Okay." He nodded back. He'd been a dad for only a few weeks, and he'd be a grandpa in a matter of months, and both notions seemed outrageous to him. Yet, when he looked at Kelly, his heart stirred in a way it never had before, and he knew God had given her to him. He'd walk through whatever they had to walk through. She was his wife, and the two were one flesh in the eyes of his Lord and Savior.

He looked around the kitchen. "What can I do to help?"

"Well, Sadie is already setting the table. Zoey made a salad. You can get that out of the fridge."

He raised his eyebrows. "Zoey did?"

Kelly smiled. "Mmm-hmm." She looked at his clothes and frowned. "But before you touch any of this food, you need to change your clothes."

Harold grinned and kissed the tip of her nose. "I'll be back in a sec."

As he made his way to the bedroom, he noticed Cam in the backyard making a snowman with Brittany, Candy, and Ellie. "Where's Zoey?"

"In her bedroom. Getting ready," Kelly called from the kitchen.

Harold undressed and jumped into the shower. *How did a teenage girl get ready to tell her family she was pregnant?* He needed to find something else to think about. Finishing his shower, he got out and saw Kelly's bottle of purple lotion on the bathroom sink. He opened the cap and inhaled the soft, flowery fragrance. *Mmm.* He loved that smell. *I love it even more when it's on her.*

Smiling, he hurried and got dressed then headed into the kitchen and busied himself with the various things Kelly asked him to do. Soon, the family, all eight of them, sat at the table.

"I'm starving, Uncle Harold. Can we eat?" Ellie asked.

Harold couldn't get over the fact that the almost seven-year-old called him Uncle Harold. He loved the endearment and secretly wished the girls would one day want to call him Dad. It was probably a selfish wish. They'd had a dad, a really good one from everything he'd heard about Tim. He should just be thankful for the opportunity to be a father figure to them, and yet. . .

He pushed the thought aside. "Let me say blessing first, okay, Ellie?"

She nodded, and the family bowed their heads.

"Dear Lord, thank You for our food. Thank You for Kelly, Sadie, and Zoey preparing it."

Sitting beside him, Zoey stiffened at the mention of her name.

He went on. "Bless this food to the nourishment of our bodies. Bless our time together as a family."

His mind whirled as his usual prayer felt stilted and cold His spirit stirred with feeling for this family, his family.

"God, thank You for my family, these people You've blessed me with. I love them, Lord."

Zoey shifted again at his left. Kelly grabbed his hand at his right and squeezed. Emotion threatened to overwhelm him, just as it had the day of the wedding.

"I love them all, sweet Lord. Amen."

"Amen," the family echoed, and Harold looked at Kelly. Her eyes brimmed with the hint of tears, and Harold couldn't help but smile at his sweet, sensitive wife. She'd cried more in the last month then she had in the year he'd known her, but he would help see her through. If she would let him.

Once they'd almost finished their meal of salad and Kelly's famous homemade lasagna, Kelly clasped her hands together. "Well, family, we have an announcement to make."

"You're pregnant!" Sadie exclaimed, looking from Kelly to Harold.

Harold burst out laughing. "No!" The idea was ludicrous. He couldn't even begin to imagine being a dad of teen girls, a grandpa, and a dad to a newborn all at the same time. He smacked his hand against the table and looked at Kelly. "Could you imagine?" He pointed from himself to her. "Me and you having a baby."

"Harold!" Kelly squealed. "I'm not sure how to take what you're implying. Are you saying I'm old?"

Harold frowned. His ire rose, as did his voice. "How could

that possibly be about me saying you're old? Do you think we need a baby right now?"

Her face reddened. "No. I don't think we need a baby right now, but I don't like you implying I'm getting old, especially when. . ."

Tears welled in her eyes. Harold rolled his eyes. The waterworks. At that moment, he found himself sick of the waterworks. He knew he was being a jerk, but suddenly he didn't want to comfort his wife.

"I'm sorry," Sadie said. "I didn't mean—"

"It's not your fault," Zoey interrupted. "They're freaking out because it's my fault. I'm the one who's pregnant."

❧

Kelly laid her head down on her desk. It had been a long evening at her house last night, with Sadie zipping Zoey off to another room, and she and Harold answering all of Brittany's and Candy's questions. Then there was a lot of silence. Stunned silence was the only thing she knew to call it.

The day at school had been equally trying. A fight broke out in the hall in front of her room. Kelly had never been more thankful to have a classroom beside the oversized male science teacher. Her computer quit working twice during her PowerPoint presentation and an array of other "little" things kept going wrong. Now, she rested her head on the paper she needed to sign to allow Zoey to be a homebound student for the rest of the year.

This wasn't what Kelly wanted for her daughter. Zoey would miss prom and basketball games and the senior trip. She didn't even want to walk at graduation.

A light knock sounded against the frame of her classroom door. She lifted her head and saw Cam walking toward her.

"Don't you look a sight?" He thumped her forehead with his middle finger.

"Ouch." She pushed his hand away and scowled at him. "What are you doing here?"

"Come to talk to you."

She leaned back in her chair. "Didn't we all do enough talking to last us a lifetime last night?"

Cam sat on the top of one of her student desks, clasping his hands in his lap. "Sadie's worried for Zoey."

"Me, too."

"We prayed over her a long time last night. Sadie mentioned she saw a bit of a change in her when she talked to her. For the good."

"I hope Sadie's right. Zoey needs God now more than ever."

"So do you."

Kelly sat up in her chair. She leaned over, placing her elbows across her desk. "I know. Clinging to Him is the only way we'll get through this."

"And Harold will help."

Kelly didn't respond. She reached for her earring, fiddling the coarse prongs between her fingertips, she twisted it forward and then back.

"I knew it." Cam smacked his hands together.

Kelly frowned. "What?"

"I wasn't sure if you were struggling with God or with Harold, but I knew it was one of them."

"What's that supposed to mean?"

"It means you've got to let your guard down. I could tell last night you were stiff as a two-by-four. That explains why you two got so mad over Sadie's question."

Kelly shook her head. "Oh, I hope we didn't hurt Sadie's

eelings. It wasn't about—"

"She's fine, but you're not. You and Harold can help each other through this."

Kelly turned away from her brother. How could she explain the guilt she felt every time she looked at Harold? He'd become the "Coyle women chauffeur" man. The only perk he received from the situation was having one of them share his name. She loved Harold, or at least she thought she did, but wouldn't true love keep the one they love away from heartache and trauma?

She'd thrown him into a den of lionesses.

"Why are you pushing Harold away?"

Kelly faced her brother, spreading her arms wide. "Don't you see how selfish I am? Zoey is due at the beginning of July. That's six months after our wedding. I found out she was pregnant at our reception. I had to fight through the worry every day of my honeymoon."

"That's why you should lean on your husband."

"No." Kelly shook her head. "Harold didn't sign up to be a husband, a father to three girls, and now a grandpa. He'd been a bachelor all his life, no siblings even. Don't you think my brood is a bit overwhelming for him? Why would he even want to be a part of it? I fell in love with him and didn't have the strength to let him live a peaceful life." She fell back into her chair. "I'm selfish."

Saying the words aloud heightened her despair. She'd had hinting moments before their wedding that she shouldn't force Harold into her drama, but he'd always been so kind, telling her how much he loved her and the girls.

"Big sister, I think you're nuts."

"What?" Kelly glared up at Cam.

"So, it's all your fault that Harold is forced to live in a house with four women. After all, he didn't know you had three girls the day he showed up at your house to fix your heater."

"Well, of course he knew—"

"And it wasn't him who asked you out on a date."

"He asked me, but—"

"And I suppose you were the one who asked him to marry you—I mean, as I remember we were at your house and he brought out a birthday cake and—"

"Cam, I know all that. But he didn't ask to be a grandpa."

Cam raised his eyebrows. "That's right, but you asked to be a grandma to your seventeen-year-old daughter's child."

"Cam—"

"No, you listen. Kelly, you *are* being selfish."

Kelly's heart dropped at his words. She knew they were true, but that didn't make her feel any better.

Cam continued, "But not because you married him. It's because you aren't trusting him now."

Kelly grew defensive. "I trust Harold. I can't believe you would say that."

"Do you, Kelly? If you trusted him, you'd give him some of the burden."

"But they're not his kids, Cam. It's not fair—"

"I can't believe you would say that. To me, especially."

Kelly stepped out of her own spiraling gyro of misery and looked at her brother. Cam would never be able to have biological children. Ellie would be his only child, and she was adopted, unless he and Sadie chose to adopt more. She knew her brother loved Ellie more than his own life, but Cam had chosen to adopt Ellie.

Just as Harold chose to marry me with three girls attached.

She shook her head. That's where her thinking was slanted. He didn't choose to marry her with three girls attached. He chose to be their father. He loved them. She knew he loved them. How could she have been such an idiot, so full of pride? She'd held the man she loved, who loved her, at arm's length since their wedding day.

"Cam, you're right. And I'm sorry."

A smile bowed Cam's lips. "Wow, that admission was rather quick."

Kelly shook her head at his sudden silliness. "Will you do me a favor?"

"Sure."

"Can the girls stay with you and Sadie this Friday? Harold and I need some time alone. I've got some apologizing to do."

nine

Harold wiped the sweat from his brow. It was the end of January and Delaware was experiencing record cold temperatures, but he spent most of his days swiping off sweat. It seemed to be some kind of central air trend in his area that the units were shutting down. He, Rudy, and Walt had put in long hours, day after day, and yet the calls wouldn't stop coming.

It didn't matter that he didn't have time to go home. Life was easier this way. At home, Zoey clung to Kelly, Brittany had reverted into some kind of shell, and Candy was full of questions and concerns. And for some reason, she wanted to voice all of them to Harold. He thought of the conversation they'd had the night before.

"Will Zoey still live with us when she has the baby?" Candy asked as she sat next to Harold on the couch and leaned against his arm.

"Of course," Harold answered as he put his arm around the girl who was content to allow him to be a parental figure.

"Will the baby live here?"

Harold had always assumed the child would live with them. It would be hard; definitely more than he'd ever anticipated before marrying Kelly, but he assumed they'd take care of the child. "Well, yes."

"Will I get to hold the baby?" Her voice took on an excited lilt.

"Sure."

"And change her and feed her and—"

"I'd say you'll get to do plenty of that."

Candy's gaze dropped, and her tone changed. "The baby won't have a daddy. Zoey said she can't find her boyfriend."

Harold swallowed anew at the remembrance of the change in the discussion. "That's true, but I'll help with the baby, too."

"It's not the same."

Harold shook his head. The memory of the words tore his heart even now. He thought of the girls and how they'd been without their dad, Tim, for nearly four years. Four years was a long time, and they'd been very close to their dad.

He knew he probably shouldn't, but part of him, if he were honest, a big part of him, was jealous that he "wasn't the same" as having Tim in their lives. He could never take their father's place.

And yet he wanted to.

Having finally finished the last central air unit of the day, Harold dropped the last few tools into his toolbox. *God, I shouldn't be jealous of Tim. And I haven't been until just recently. Why, God? Why now?*

He knew the answer. Kelly wasn't the same since Zoey had told her about the pregnancy. He knew she wouldn't be. Wouldn't expect her to even pretend to be. What mother was happy when her seventeen-year-old daughter told her that she was pregnant? He had zero experience with babies, but he wasn't so dumb as to not understand that babies changed everything.

But it was the kind of change in Kelly that hurt him to the core of his being. It was as if she didn't want to lean on him for help. Didn't trust him enough to help. For a man who'd spent his entire adult life proving to people that he was a man of integrity, a man of honor, to have his wife not trust him, not be willing to allow him to help her in her time of need— well, it shattered his very existence.

How many times had he heard her almost-silent weeping against her pillow at night? He would try to draw her near to him, but the tears would stop and she would become rigid as a metal pipe. When he hugged or kissed her or even tried to hold her in his arms for only a moment, Kelly's gaze clouded and her body language screamed of a wall she'd built to keep him out.

So, he'd quit trying. They'd been married just a little over month, and he'd spent the last two weeks focused on his work—even when he could have gone home.

Candy's words slithered into his mind again. "*It's not the same.*" *Would Kelly have welcomed Tim's touch? Would she have allowed him to comfort her and soothe her through the anxiety and worry?*

Forgive me for thinking this way, Lord. The last thing Harold wanted to do was dishonor the memory of a man he didn't even know. But he didn't want to battle a ghost, either. He wanted Kelly to allow Harold to be her husband now, to love him and honor him, for better or for worse. She had to trust him with the worst.

But she didn't.

And for now, working long, hard hours over a heating unit or a plumbing system was much easier.

❧

Friday's finally here. Kelly slipped out from under the covers. Harold had left for work two hours before. She didn't know how the man could get up before five every day, but today she was thankful. He wouldn't know she'd taken a personal day from school to prepare a special evening with him.

After waking the girls up, she made a list of everything she wanted to get accomplished today. She'd drop the girls off at school, Zoey would spend the day with Cam, and Sadie would take the younger ones home with her afterward, so Kelly didn't have to worry about any problems with them. Then, Kelly would get her nails done, toenails, too, because she wanted to look extra special for Harold tonight. It made her laugh that her simple man loved her bright pink toenail polish, but paid no attention at all to her fingernails.

After that, she would go to the store, then maybe run by the department store to pick up something special to wear. When he returned home from work, Harold would be overwhelmed by a candlelit dinner and an evening for just the two of them.

Dear God, I can hardly wait. Please let tonight be wonderful. I haven't given Harold my whole heart lately. Forgive me, Lord.

"Mom," Zoey whined as she walked into Kelly's bedroom. "I don't feel good this morning."

"Go get some ginger ale and eat a cracker."

"I don't want to go to Cam's house today."

Kelly pursed her lips. Zoey's clinging had almost become unbearable, and though it was always tempting to give in to her girls when they didn't feel well, Kelly knew she and Harold needed this evening together. "Sorry, Zoey. You can rest at Cam's just as easily as you can rest here. But while you're resting, you have to do your schoolwork for today."

"Mom," Zoey whined and placed her hand over her stomach, "I really don't think I can do it. I feel so bad."

"You have to."

"But, I—"

"No buts. You're going to be a mom soon. You have to learn to keep going, even when you don't feel like it."

"Mom. . ."

Kelly looked her daughter in the eye. "I mean it."

Tears pooled in Zoey's eyes. "I never asked to get pregnant. Why does everything bad happen to me?"

"'For the wages of sin is death, but the gift of God is eternal life.' Zoey, I know you don't like when I preach to you, and I'm not. But the truth is you sinned. Now, you have consequences. Babies are a blessing, and we will love this baby, but you have to seek God's forgiveness. You need Him now more then ever."

Kelly expected Zoey to explode, to tell Kelly that she didn't want to hear about God and what He could do for her. Instead, Zoey was silent. Kelly couldn't tell if she thought about what Kelly had said or if she'd completely tuned Kelly out, but Zoey turned and walked out of the room. Once Kelly finished dressing and went into the living room, all three girls were ready. No one, including Zoey, had anything to say as they drove to school and then to Cam's.

After Zoey stepped out of the car, Kelly opened her cell phone and called Harold. His deep voice sounded over the line when he picked it up, and Kelly felt a twinge of excitement zing through her veins. "Hey, hun."

"Aren't you supposed to be at school?" His voice sounded confused, and she looked at the clock on the dash. *What was I thinking calling him right now? I should be getting ready to start first period.* So anxious about the evening, Kelly had just wanted to hear his voice, to be sure he was coming home for dinner.

"Uh. . .class is about to start." She grinned. She hadn't lied. She just hadn't said that she wasn't there. "I just wanted to be sure you would be home for dinner tonight."

"Yeah, I'll be home. Why? No one has practice tonight, do they?"

Kelly cringed at his question. Since they got married, Harold had become the practice-chauffeur king. He never seemed to mind, but again she wondered at the fairness of marrying him when she knew how hectic her life was day in and day out. *Stop it*, she inwardly fussed at herself. *Remember what Cam said. Harold knew about the chaos, and he still wanted to marry me. Just love him, and stop feeling so guilty.*

"No," she said. "No practices today. I was just planning to cook tonight and wanted to be sure you'd be able to get home."

"Yep, I'll be there. I'll see you tonight."

"I love you, Harold."

A moment of silence wrapped around her after she said those words. How long had it been since she'd told her new husband she loved him—a couple of weeks, maybe—and they'd only been married a little over a month. Her heart ached at her foolishness. *God, forgive me. Help me show Harold how much I love and appreciate him.*

"I love you, too, Kelly. So much." Harold's voice sounded somber and serious, and Kelly's heart pained at the tone. She clicked the phone off and gazed at herself in the rearview mirror. *Tonight will be special. No more pushing Harold away. No more feeling guilty for making his life crazy. I'm simply going to love him.*

Hours later, Kelly stomped the snow off her boots before she walked into the house. In addition to having her nails done, she'd also gotten her hair cut and colored. The style was quite flattering and a bit sassy, and she couldn't wait to see Harold that evening. She glanced at the clock. She waited five more minutes so she could call Harold without him wondering what she was doing. She clicked his number again. After only one ring, his deep voice resonated over the line, sending a thrill down her spine again.

"Hey. How has your day been?" she asked.

"Believe it or not, kinda slow."

She peered outside. The sun shone bright, glistening against the snow-covered ground. "I wouldn't think there would be any central heating units in the state left to fix. You've worked a lot lately."

Harold chuckled. "I think you're right."

"So, when will you be home?"

"I'd say five—five thirty."

Kelly looked at the clock again. That gave her two hours to prepare filet mignon, baked potatoes, fresh rolls, and whip up a salad.

"What's for dinner?" Harold's voice interrupted her thoughts.

"It's a surprise."

Harold laughed. "Okay. Just make sure Brittany doesn't eat it all before I get home."

Kelly smiled at the joke Harold and Brittany often bantered over. Her nearly six-foot-tall daughter, who was as big around as a twig, could eat every bit as much as Harold, and they loved to compete to see who could eat the most. "Don't worry about that. I'll see you tonight. I love you."

"Love you, too."

He clicked off and Kelly set to work. She took out the filets, seasoned them, and secured bacon around the steaks with toothpicks. She washed and scrubbed the potatoes and wrapped them in aluminum foil. With the meat and potatoes cooking in the oven, she mixed Harold's favorite ingredients for salad. She glanced at the clock again. *He'll be here in an hour.*

Finishing in the kitchen quickly, she picked up the fresh red roses she'd purchased, tore off the petals, and allowed them to fall in various places. She changed into the new outfit she'd purchased, then took the food from the oven. After setting the table with care, she glanced at the clock on the microwave. He would be home any minute. She lit the candles. *God, bless our evening together.*

૭ë

Harold trudged up the sidewalk toward the house. It was nine o'clock, and he was beat. Just before he was heading home for the night, a woman called. Her pipes had burst. Walt hadn't been able to stay to help, but Harold and Rudy spent the last four hours working at the woman's house. Kelly had called six times or more before he'd finally had the chance to answer and tell her what was going on. She sounded a little strange on the phone, but Harold figured Zoey was just driving Kelly crazy.

His favorite apple-cinnamon scent assaulted him as he opened the front door. The lights were off, but as he walked toward the kitchen, he saw the dining room table was set for two. Candles that looked to have been lit for hours, but were now dark, sat in the middle of the table. Rose petals covered the floor. Realization dawned on him and his heart dropped. *She planned a special evening for us.*

He strode into the kitchen, opened the refrigerator, and noted the filet mignon and baked potato wrapped in cellophane. Regret wrapped around him as he followed the rose petals down the hall. He should have answered her calls. He should have come home. They could have rigged the woman's pipes until the morning. He didn't have to fix them completely.

Standing in the bedroom door, he took in his beautiful wife curled up in the bed. She gripped a pillow at her chest. He could only see her profile, but he could tell her makeup had smeared down her cheek. *From crying, because I didn't come home.*

Slowly, he made his way toward the bed, then gently sat beside her. He leaned over and kissed her forehead. She jumped, her eyes widening in fear.

He stroked her hair. "I'm sorry, Kelly."

Her expression softened, and he was surprised to see she wasn't angry. "I'm sorry, too, Harold. I've been unfair to you."

"I should have come home."

Kelly smiled. She reached up and traced her fingers through his hair. "You're home now."

Contentment filled his heart. "I love you, Kelly."

She sat up. "I know you do, and from here on out, I'm going to let you."

The comment washed over him like a soothing balm. She trusted him. She would lean on him. He would be the husband he wanted to be, the one she needed him to be. And, he wouldn't let her down.

ten

A week passed since Kelly had let down her guard, and Harold enjoyed every moment of sensitivity. He hadn't realized just how emotional Kelly had become since finding out Zoey was pregnant. The woman cried at the drop of a hat, and her stomach often felt queasy. But now she allowed Harold to comfort her. At night she nestled into his arms and allowed him to pray over their family. They also spent time in the mornings sharing what God had shown them in His Word, and he'd grown to treasure the beginnings and endings of each day. Sure, he got to work thirty minutes later than he used to, but most people didn't head out before six a.m. The extra half hour wouldn't hurt the community or his business.

He walked up behind Kelly, wrapped his arms around her, and kissed the back of her head. "I had an idea this morning."

"Well, I have to be at work in forty-five minutes and I haven't fixed my hair."

She winked at him, and he chuckled. "I was thinking I'd take Zoey shopping today."

Kelly's eyes widened. "What?"

"She can do her homebound schoolwork when we get home. I'll probably only make it until after lunch anyway, but I'd like to take her to get some maternity clothes."

Kelly placed her hands on her hips. "You want to take Zoey to buy clothes—maternity clothes?" Her tone dripped with sarcasm and confusion.

"Well, of course I don't want to take her. I just think she

needs—I don't know. She's still clinging to you a lot, and every time I pray, she remains heavy on my heart. I just think maybe I should. . .let her know I'll help her and the baby in any way I can."

Kelly stared at him for a moment, then tears welled in her eyes. *Oh boy, here come the waterworks again.* She wrapped her arms around Harold's neck. "I think that's a great idea. You're the best man"—she pressed her lips to his in a quick motion—"in the whole world."

Harold laughed and kissed her back. "Okay. Guess I need to tell Zoey."

"I'll tell her."

Kelly zipped out of the room. He could hear her and Zoey talking. Zoey didn't sound as excited, but he heard her consent to go. He put on his shoes and grabbed a quick breakfast. To his surprise, Zoey was ready to go.

"Where are we going?" Zoey asked as she buckled her seat belt.

"To the Concord Mall. Does that sound okay?"

Zoey nodded and looked out the windshield. The drive was a quiet one, and Harold was thankful when they finally made it to their destination. Silently, they walked into the mall. She looked up at him. "Where should we go?"

"You lead the way. I'm just here to pay for what you need." He laughed, trying to lighten the tension. She stared at him, but her expression wasn't hard as it once had been. Instead, it was a mixture of sadness and age. Zoey had changed so much since the pregnancy. She no longer argued. She helped out around the house without being asked. She'd allowed her hair to go back to her natural, auburn shade. But she still clung to her sadness. *Please, God, draw her back to Yourself.*

Harold followed Zoey to several stores. At the first one she picked up a few items without trying them on. The new clothes seemed to lighten her step a bit, and at the next store she asked if he minded if she tried on a few of the shirts before they bought them. Harold walked dutifully through each store, trying not to compare shopping to eating a metal pipe. He pulled out his debit card when it was needed then moved along behind Zoey.

"What do you think of this shirt?"

Harold hoped he masked the shock on his face when Zoey asked his opinion. He knew with each hour she loosened up a bit, making small comments, saying thank you at appropriate times. Now she was asking what he thought. He knew he'd never take the place of her father, but he wanted to make his own place in her life. *God, maybe I am making some progress with Zoey.* "It looks great. You should get two."

Zoey giggled, and for the first time in a long time, the smile reached her eyes. "I only need one." She placed her hand on her stomach. "I'm starving. Can we go eat after this?"

"Definitely." Harold looked at his watch. He thought he was going to have to eat his fist. Shopping was exhausting, and he'd worked off his measly bowl of cereal two hours ago.

He bought the items she'd selected, and they headed toward the food court. After ordering, picking up their food, and finding a table, Harold sat across from Zoey and nodded. "Wanna pray?"

"You can."

Harold bowed his head. "Lord, thank You for this day with Zoey. I've had a good time with her. Let this food nourish her and the baby. Amen."

Harold glanced up and noticed Zoey studied her food.

"Thanks for taking me today, Harold," she mumbled without looking up.

"Not a problem." He motioned toward the food. "Now, feed that baby."

Zoey chuckled, picked up a fry, and stuck it in her mouth. "You know, Mom really loves you."

Harold took a slow bite of his sandwich. He hadn't expected Zoey to open up to him; he'd just wanted to let her know he was there for her. "I love your mom, too."

"She loved my dad, as well."

Harold swallowed slowly then wiped his mouth with a napkin. "I know she did. I think your dad must have been a really special guy."

"He was."

Zoey grew quiet as she took several bites of her sandwich. Harold tried not to watch as she chewed and took sips of her soft drink. He could tell in his spirit she had more to say. He wanted to encourage her, but no words would come to him. He wasn't good with words anyway. He'd always been more of a listener, and his experience with women was minimal at best. Though dating and marrying Kelly had changed that quite a bit.

"I've been so mad at God." Zoey's words were soft, and she still hadn't looked up from her tray. "I said really ugly things to Him when Daddy died. I told Him I hated Him."

Zoey looked up then, peering into Harold's eyes. Harold gripped his napkin between his fingers. *God, give me the right words to say.* "I know you don't hate God."

Tears pooled in Zoey's eyes, and she didn't bother to brush them away. Her gaze stayed focused on Harold's. "I don't. I don't hate God."

She looked back down at her food. She stuck a french fry

in ketchup and twirled it around. "When I was doing stuff I shouldn't have been doing, I would come home at night and yell at God in my mind."

She dropped the fry and grabbed her straw and twirled it around. "I would tell Him that in Romans He said that nothing could separate me from His love."

"Romans 8:38–39." Harold said the scripture. He'd just read the verses only weeks before. They'd stuck with him because he'd thought of Zoey and how he wanted to make her see that God loved her so much.

The tears streamed down her cheeks. This time she brushed them away with her napkin. "Yes. That's right. I told Him He had to love me. He couldn't give up on me."

Harold reached over and squeezed her hand. "He hasn't given up on you, Zoey."

Zoey sniffed and looked up at the ceiling. "I don't want to yell at Him anymore."

"He'll forgive you."

"I know."

Harold waited as Zoey wiped her face with her napkin then started to eat her lunch again. His heart drummed in his chest. He knew something had changed within her. But what was he supposed to say to her? Nothing would come. No words. No great comment of wisdom. Some father figure he was. He took a drink then finished his lunch, praying for God to show him what he could say. Nothing. He wasn't hearing anything.

Harold and Zoey walked out to his truck. He placed her bags behind their seats. He started to hop into the cab when he felt Zoey beside him. Before he could say a word, she wrapped her arms around him. Stunned, Harold hesitantly returned her hug. "Thank you, Harold."

"You're welcome."

Harold patted her back then hopped into the truck. Zoey walked around to the passenger's side and jumped in as well. "God's forgiven me, Harold."

Harold smiled as he placed the key in the ignition. "Of course He has."

"I can feel His forgiveness, but it's not because I can feel it that I know He has. He says He has in His Word. If I confess my sins, He is faithful and just to forgive my sins and cleanse me from my unrighteousness." She shrugged. " 'Course, I said it in my own words."

"You know, I think you came pretty close to what the scripture actually says. Isn't that from First John?"

"Yep. Chapter one, verse 9. If I remember right, that book talks a whole lot about God's love."

Harold peered at his stepdaughter. "You know an awful lot about the Bible, young lady."

Zoey grumbled. "You would, too, if you grew up with my mom."

"Sounds like she's a pretty good mom."

"She is."

Without thinking, Harold reached over and ruffled Zoey's hair. He pulled his hand back, realizing she was too old for the gesture. Zoey laughed and punched his arm. Harold feigned pain. "I'm telling your mother."

Zoey's expression became serious. "Let me tell her about today."

"I wouldn't have it any other way." Harold stared out the windshield as they headed home. *She's finally beginning to heal. Thank You, Lord.*

Kelly's stomach churned as she made her way into her classroom. She plopped into her chair and laid her head on her desk. Three of her students had been out with the flu in the last few days. She feared she'd caught the bug from them. But *I took my temperature this morning, and it was normal.*

She forced herself to lift her head and take a sip of the lemon-lime soda she'd purchased in the teacher's lounge. The lack of a fever meant nothing. She and all three of her girls were notorious for not running temperatures when they were sick. Taking slow, deep breaths, Kelly turned her rolling chair toward her computer and turned it on. She had a busy day today—team meeting with the principal during plan, a parent meeting over an at-risk-of-failing student after school. Plus she was starting *Hamlet* with her accelerated classes today. She didn't have time to be sick.

She took another quick sip of soda, then pulled a few saltine crackers out of her bag. She nibbled on a few, thankful her stomach seemed to settle just a bit. She had to get the students' warm-ups on the board before they started down the hallway. She forced herself to get up, walk to the board, and write down their daily prompt.

The bell rang, and Kelly heard the stampede of teenagers making their way down the hall. Her stomach rumbled again, and Kelly headed for the bathroom. She grabbed a paper towel and ran cool water over it. Trying not to mess up her makeup, she dabbed the towel against her neck and jaw. She let out a long breath. *I can do this. I can make it through the day.*

She walked out of the bathroom, down the hall, and into her room. The final bell hadn't rung, and students sat on top of desks and stood in clusters around the room. Someone had brought a cup of coffee to class, as she allowed them to have drinks until the final bell, but the smell sent her stomach into a whirl once again. Not to mention the various colognes and perfumes that mingled in the air. Normally, she didn't mind the smell, but today. . .

She scooped her soda off the desk and took a sip. *Once the day gets going, I'll be fine.* Trying not to push her stomach too far, she sat in her chair and opened the attendance page on her computer.

"Ms. Coyle—I mean, Smith," one of her students began. "I forgot my homework at my dad's house, and I stayed at my mom's house last night."

Kelly looked at the tiny brunette. The girl never uttered a peep in class and was a straight-A student, but through her writing, Kelly had learned her parents' divorce had been a bitter one and it had taken a toll on the teen.

"And my mom wouldn't take me over to my dad's this morning, because. . ." She looked down. "Well, if I had my license, I could—"

Kelly shook her head. "Don't worry about it. You can bring it to me tomorrow."

The girl smiled, exposing dimples that made her look five years younger. "Thanks, Mrs. Smith."

As she walked away, the floral scent of her perfume wrapped itself around Kelly, turning her stomach. She bit into another cracker.

Logan, one of her sweetest and most talkative students approached her desk. "How's your morning going, Mrs. S.?"

The strong aroma of coffee smacked her in the face. She looked at his hand that carried the oversized cup of joe. The churning of her stomach whirled like a tornado. A hot flash washed over her body. Kelly grabbed her mouth and ran for the door. Bile rose in her mouth. She couldn't make it.

She spied the trash can beside her door. She gripped the sides as her body hurled.

"Gross," a feminine voice sounded behind her.

"That was awesome," another voice sounded.

"Mrs. S., are you okay?" Logan stood beside her. He'd placed his hand on her back. The boy meant well. He was such a sweet kid, but at the moment, she wished he'd take a few steps away from her.

"Here you go." Logan handed her a tissue.

Maybe she was glad to have him there after all. She took the tissue and wiped her mouth. "Thanks, Logan." She picked up the trash can and set it in the hall. "Will you call the office, please? We need a custodian, and I think I need a sub."

The principal sent her home before the sub arrived. He covered her class for her. She thanked God all the way home that she worked for such a wonderful man. The custodian had been so sweet to her, as well. Decked out in his plastic gloves, he wouldn't let Kelly help clean up her mess. She felt weak as a cooked spaghetti noodle and green as basil. The thought of Italian food sent her stomach to spinning again. *Lord, I don't want the flu.*

She pulled into her driveway and walked into the house. She just needed to sleep for a little bit. Without any overwhelming smells or noises or anything of that nature, she would be able to rest and then be ready to go the next day. She had to be ready the next day.

Using every ounce of energy she could muster, Kelly slipped out of her clothes and into a flannel nightgown. She crawled beneath the covers of her bed and curled up a pillow and pressed it gently against her stomach. She took slow, cleansing breaths and closed her eyes.

"Kelly, are you okay?"

Kelly startled at a coarse hand rubbing her cheek. She opened her eyes and saw the worried expression on Harold's face. "I think I have the flu."

"Oh, honey." He continued to stroke her face. "You don't feel warm."

"I know, but I never run a fever." She tried to sit up. Her stomach no longer felt queasy, and she realized she wanted something to eat. "What time is it?"

"One o'clock. Zoey's fixing some chicken noodle soup for you."

"That sounds wonderful." Embarrassment flooded her as she thought of her morning. "I threw up at school. In front of everyone."

Harold grinned. "I bet the kids loved that."

"I gave them something to talk about today, that's for sure."

Harold kissed her forehead. "I'm going to head in to work for a little while. You rest today."

"I will."

Kelly slipped out of bed and made her way to the bathroom. She felt so much better than she had this morning. She didn't even feel sick. Maybe it was just a quick bug. Kelly had found over the years that she seldom got as sick as her students. She figured her body had built a good immune system through working with so many teenagers.

Kelly walked into the kitchen and grabbed the bowl of soup Zoey had fixed for her. She sat at the small breakfast table. "Thanks."

"You're welcome." Zoey sat across from her. "How are you feeling?"

"I'll be fine. Just a bug, I'm sure. You better not get to close to me."

"I won't." Zoey grinned, and Kelly noted something had changed in her daughter. Her smile met her eyes for the first time since Tim died.

"How was your shopping trip with Harold?"

"Great. He bought me a lot of stuff."

"You want to show me?"

"Not right now. Mom. . ."

Kelly watched her oldest child. Zoey's light blue eyes shone with peace. Her hair, no longer a much-too-dark shade hung in auburn waves past her shoulders. The freckles that splattered her nose gave her a youthful look, but the swelling of her belly was proof that Zoey would grow up whether she was ready or not. But Zoey had grown up so much since Tim's death, even more since her pregnancy. Kelly knew the bitterness Zoey struggled with had been subsiding over the last few months. She'd prayed constantly for Zoey's reconciliation with God.

"Mom, I've made peace with God."

Bliss, pure and profound, poured over Kelly like a rush of water. She closed her eyes, allowing the answer to her heart's deepest prayer for the last three years to penetrate her soul. *Praise You, Jesus. Praise You.*

"I still don't know why God let Daddy die."

Kelly grabbed her daughter's hand. "I don't either, sweetie."

"But I know all things work together for good—"

"To those who love God." Kelly finished part of the scripture. "You've been reading Romans?"

Zoey shrugged. "I read through Romans a few weeks ago after my homework one day. Besides, you used to say that scripture all the time after Daddy died."

"I didn't know you were listening."

"I listen, even when you don't think I am."

Kelly studied her daughter. Contentment wrapped her features, and Kelly could hardly hold back her shouts of praise to the Lord. *Why hold it back?* "Praise the Lord!" she shouted.

Zoey jumped and placed her hand on her chest. "Mom, you scared the life out of me."

Kelly stood up and walked around the table. She embraced her oldest child, her firstborn. "Zoey, your life is back in you. And that is reason to shout."

eleven

It had been over a week since Kelly had gotten sick at school, and she was still battling the virus. She'd never run a fever, but her stomach would settle for only a few hours a day, her body ached, and the fatigue was nearly debilitating. Daily, she barely made it in the door from school before she'd hit the couch.

Harold had been sweet, taking the girls where they needed to go, doing some of the laundry. And Zoey had been doing most of the cooking, but tonight they were planning a movie outing, and Kelly wanted to fix a nice lasagna dinner for the family. Willing herself to feel better, she dumped the hamburger into a skillet and let it start cooking. She quickly diced an onion and green pepper and mixed them in with the cooking meat. The smell, one she normally loved, filled her nostrils, and Kelly gagged.

This is ridiculous. I refuse to be sick any longer. Praying for strength she got out the tomato sauce, tomato paste, and various spices to make the sauce. She ignored her body's protests to the food and continued cooking until the lasagna was covered in aluminum foil and placed in the oven.

"Girls, you need to get ready," Kelly called through the house as she headed toward the bathroom. "We're leaving after dinner."

"Harold said we could go to my movie," Candy said as she walked into Kelly's room.

"I know."

"I can't wait to see Harold's face when it starts," Zoey called

123

from the other room.

"Me, too," Brittany added.

Candy placed her hands on her hips. "All of my friends have gone to see it. It's supposed to be a good movie."

Kelly smiled. "I'm sure it is." She patted Candy's shoulder. "I think your sisters just find it humorous that Harold is going to watch a musical about high school students."

Kelly's stomach rumbled. The smell of frying hamburger meat mixed with onions and green peppers seemed to cling to her. "I'm going to take my bath," she said to Candy, determined not to show her family that she still felt sick. Besides the next day was Valentine's, and she knew Harold had a special dinner planned for the two of them. She had to feel better.

She started the hot water then pulled a towel and washrag from the cabinet. She slinked into the tub, hoping the water would soothe her nausea as it had the past several days. Lying all the way back, she closed her eyes and relished the warm water. Grabbing the timer beside the tub, she turned it to fifteen minutes. By then, she knew her stomach would be all right.

As she expected, the soak helped, and Kelly dressed and fixed up for dinner and a movie. She knew Harold had gotten home; she could hear him talking to the girls in the other room. She opened the bedroom door and saw Harold sitting beside Zoey at the table. They'd discovered that her simple man was quite adept at numbers, and he often helped the girls with their math, especially Zoey since she was homebound.

"I don't understand this part," Zoey said.

"Remember. You have to use this formula." Harold pointed to the book. "You punch it into the calculator like this."

Kelly leaned against the doorframe and watched her daughter pay attention to every word Harold said. The teen had done a full one-eighty since she'd recommitted herself to the Lord. Her belly had blossomed just a bit, and it would be only a matter of weeks before she'd have an ultrasound. Kelly prayed Zoey's faith would stay strong after the birth of the child. It had been difficult enough to have a baby at twenty with a husband. Zoey would only be eighteen without a father present at all.

"Harold, I need help when you're done with Zoey," Brittany said as she walked up beside them.

Harold grimaced, and Kelly remembered he'd said Brittany's Algebra II class was the hardest material for him to figure out. "I hope I can help you. I thought that boy was helping."

"Micah's a jerk," Brittany growled as she flopped into the chair beside Harold. "He kept calling me Amazon Girl today, even after I told him to stop."

Kelly watched as Harold patted her hand and said, "I think he's flirting with you."

"No he's not. He's a jerk."

No one had noticed Kelly yet, and she drank in the interaction between her husband and daughters. *God, Harold is such a blessing.*

"Hey, Harold." Candy skipped to the table and wrapped her arm around Harold's shoulder. "Mom says the movie starts at seven thirty. I can't wait."

"Me neither," Harold murmured, and Kelly almost burst into laughter. She knew the man would rather have his teeth pulled than see that movie. But he'd do it for Candy. Just as any dad would.

In due time, Harold would be the one who'd walk the girls

down the aisle to their waiting fiancés. He would be the grandfather to their children. He'd be the one they'd turn to for advice or help. Like Zoey, she didn't understand why Tim died, and she'd never want to take away from his memory. *But thank You, God, for bringing Harold into our lives. He's such a blessing.*

"Penny for your thoughts."

Kelly looked at Harold. She'd been so engrossed in her prayer she hadn't realized he'd noticed her watching them. She strolled to the table and kissed the top of his head. "I was just thinking about how thankful I am to have you."

Zoey and Candy rolled their eyes, while Brittany made a gagging motion. Kelly pointed at Zoey's homework. "Especially since you can do math."

"That's true." Brittany nodded. "We definitely need you for the math. But that's it."

"Oh really." Harold jumped out of his chair and grabbed Brittany in a headlock. She squealed as he rubbed her head with his knuckles. "Tell me I'm wonderful." He continued to rub her head. "Come on."

Candy giggled and tried to jump on Harold's back. Brittany squealed even louder. Kelly and Zoey bent over in laughter.

"Your sister's trying to help you, but she can't take me." He continued to rub Brittany's head. "Come on, Britt, tell Harold he's the bestest. Nobody's as good as Harold."

"Fine. You're the best," Brittany squealed.

"I can't hear you." Harold rubbed her head again.

"You're the best, you big meanie."

Harold let her go, and Brittany punched his arm. "Look at my hair."

"My turn," Candy yelled, and Harold wrapped her up in a

headlock and rubbed her head.

The oven timer went off. Kelly wiped the tears of laughter from her eyes as she walked into the kitchen. "Okay, you bunch of monkeys, it's time to eat."

"Mmm, food." Harold let go of Candy and pounded his chest with his fists. "Monkey hungry."

Zoey shook her head, and Harold messed her hair a bit, as well. Again, Kelly praised God for her family.

&

Harold nearly fell out of the chair when Kelly walked into the living room. His bride of less than two months stood before him wearing an all-black, silky dress. Two tiny straps touched her shoulders and held the fabric in place. The neck scooped down, but in a way that didn't show the world any of her chest. The skirt kind of flowed at the bottom, touching her knees when she walked. *Wow, she has great legs.*

He looked back at her face, noting the pleasure in her gaze. She liked that she had this kind of effect on him. He drank in her dark hair, piled up on the top of her head in a messy way that was so attractive. Little strands of hair rested on her neck, and he longed to switch places with one of those strands.

She touched the diamond necklace that rested perfectly in the center of her neck. He noticed her neck kind of glittered. In fact, her arms and legs even seemed to shine. But it wasn't just the glitter, Kelly looked fuller somehow. It was as if she were glowing in the most beautiful way.

"Honey," Harold stood up and kissed her cheek. "You are hot," he whispered in her ear.

He noted the redness trailing up her cheek, and he loved that she still thrilled at his attraction to her. Kelly twisted the bow at her waist. "I could hardly squeeze into this dress, and I just bought it two months ago."

"It sure looks awfully good."

Candy rushed into the room, and Harold backed away from his wife. Candy whistled. "Mom, you are hot!"

Brittany walked in, as well. Harold watched as her eyes widened. "No doubt, Mom." She turned to Harold and shrugged her shoulders. "Somebody's going to have to beat the guys off Mom tonight."

Harold laughed. The younger girls proved always dramatic, and always fun to be around. He winked at the two of them. "Don't worry. I'll take care of her."

"And I'll take care of them." Zoey stepped into the living room. She looked at her mom. "You look really pretty, Mom. It's like you're glowing."

Kelly touched her collarbone. The motion sent Harold's attraction into overdrive. "I did put on some of your glitter."

"You look wonderful." Harold looked at his watch. "And our reservation is in an hour. We need to get out of here."

"Okay. Have fun," Zoey said.

"Bye, Mom. Bye, Harold," commented Brittany and Candy.

As Harold guided his bride to the door, he could hear Brittany and Candy arguing over who got the TV first. He looked at Kelly and laughed at the worried expression on her face. "Don't worry about them. They'll be fine. I gave Zoey a TV schedule for the girls to follow."

Kelly's expression softened, and she kissed his lips. "You're a good dad to them."

"I want to be."

Harold opened the car door for Kelly. Since they were going on a nicer date, he'd parked the truck in the garage and they would go in Kelly's car. He walked over to the driver's seat and slipped inside. "You do look absolutely gorgeous." He winked. "I'd be willing to skip dinner."

Kelly giggled. "Oh no. You've been excited about these reservations for weeks. We are going to The Moro Restaurant."

"I don't even know if it's any good."

"They serve steak. Filets. You'll love it. And, I can't wait to try the baked chocolate mousse. I've heard it's absolutely divine." Kelly leaned closer to him and rested her cheek on his shoulder. "It's our first Valentine's Day as husband and wife."

"I know. I can hardly believe it." He glanced at Kelly. "What did you ever see in me?"

Kelly laughed. "Are you kidding me? There's not a day that goes by that I don't praise God for giving me a man who not only loves me, but loves my crazy brood, as well."

"They're my crazy brood now, too."

"Yes, they are."

Harold watched the road signs as they approached Wilmington. All week he'd looked forward to their evening together. He glanced at his wife. Her face looked pale. He noticed her breathing in through her nose and out her mouth. She wasn't feeling well again. She'd been doing this for two weeks. "Kelly, I think you need to go to the doctor."

She shook her head. "I'm fine." She looked at him and smiled, but he could tell the smile didn't reach her eyes. "Really, I feel fine."

Harold parked the car, then walked around to open the door for Kelly. He touched her hand. Clammy. "Kelly, I know you don't want to ruin our plans, but—"

"I'm fine."

They walked into the restaurant. Live jazz music mixed

with the conversation of several couples enjoying their evening. Harold looked at the dark yellow and a-little-bit-of-orange-mixed-with-a-little-bit-of-pink walls. The color reminded him of a salmon fillet before it had been cooked. The lights and pictures were fancy, not as fancy as the Dupont Hotel, but still nothing like he'd have ever gone to if he weren't married to Kelly.

He loved the circle pattern the place had going. Several of the tables had a secluded feel to them as a large, circular molding extended about a foot from the ceiling around the table. A fancy chandelier hung from the middle. The architectural design of the place was quite interesting.

A guy, waiter, or whatever Kelly said they were called, showed them to their seats. He and Kelly settled into a booth, and the man handed them the menu for the day. The man walked away, and Harold took his wife's hands in his. He looked at her. Her color did not look good. "Kelly—"

"I'll be right back." Kelly covered her mouth and ran toward the restroom.

Harold sat back in the booth and let out a long breath. Something always seemed to happen to put a damper on their time together. *Zoey tells Kelly she's pregnant before our honeymoon. I mess up Kelly's surprise dinner. Now, she's sick. Is it always going to be like this, Lord?*

His cell phone vibrated in his pocket. The word Home flashed on the screen. Trepidation washed over him as he pushed On. "Hello."

"Harold. She's bleeding."

His heart started to race. "What?"

"It's Candy. She tripped over the rug. Hit her head. Zoey's hurling." Harold could hear screams and hacking sounds in the background. The television seemed to blare along with it.

"Slow down, Brittany. Have you put something on Candy's head?"

"Yes. A rag. But she's bleeding through it. I called Cam. He's coming."

Harold could hear her start to cry. "It's okay, Brittany. We're coming."

"Please hurry."

"Just hold the rag on Candy's head. Call me if Cam gets there first and has to take her to the hospital."

Harold raced toward the bathroom. He knocked on the door. "Kelly?"

Brittany, the most sensitive of the three, didn't handle crises well, and Harold knew the mixture of blood and vomit wouldn't be good for her to handle alone.

Kelly didn't answer, so Harold knocked one more time, then walked in. Someone was vomiting in the last stall. Thankfully, no one was in there but Kelly. "Kelly?"

"What are you doing, Harold? I'm fine."

"Candy hit her head. We've got to get home."

The door opened and an older lady walked in. She screamed when she saw Harold. He placed his hand on his chest. "Sorry, ma'am. We're leaving."

Kelly stepped out of the stall. Her face was puffy from vomiting, and some of her makeup smeared down her cheeks.

The woman frowned. She placed her hand on Kelly's and glared at Harold. "You don't have to go anywhere with him, young lady. I'll take you somewhere safe. He can find another woman to torment."

Harold rolled his eyes and looked at the ceiling. "Believe me, ma'am. I have enough women tormenting me right now."

Kelly walked to Harold. She looked at the woman. "It's okay, ma'am. He's my husband. He didn't hurt me. I've been sick."

Harold grabbed Kelly's hand and nodded to the older woman. The woman scowled at him but he ignored her. "Come on. We've got to go."

"What happened?"

"Candy must have fallen. Her head is bleeding a lot, and Zoey's throwing up."

Kelly covered her mouth with her hand. "Oh no."

"Cam's on his way to the house. They're going to call if she needs stitches or anything."

"Oh no."

Harold guided Kelly toward the car. She didn't move as fast as he would have expected. He could hear her taking deep breaths. Reaching the car, he pulled out his keys.

"Oh no," Kelly mumbled again. She turned away from him and vomited in the space beside their car.

Kelly was vomiting. Zoey was vomiting. Brittany was panicking. And Candy was bleeding. *So, this was life with a bunch of women?* Being a bachelor had definitely been easier. Not that he didn't love his girls. He loved each and every one of them. Whether they were happy, sad, laughing, crying, puking, bleeding. They were his girls, and he loved them.

twelve

Kelly rested her elbows on the bar of the grocery cart. It had been a long day. Zoey had called several times asking about her schoolwork. Two more boys had gotten into a fight in her room. What is it with the boys and fighting this year? The nurse from Candy's school had called to let Kelly know she'd given her daughter pain reliever for her head. It was only four o'clock, and Kelly was ready to call it a night.

Willing herself to keep going, she stood to her full height and made her way toward the antiobiotic cream. Candy's head wound three days before had resulted in a trip to the emergency room, but thankfully, only required three stitches and a regimen of cream application. Kelly frowned as she thought about the ugly bruise surrounding the cut above Candy's eyebrow. Harold had been the one tending the wound. It was true that when Tim was alive he took care of all the girls' cuts and scrapes, but since his death Kelly had played family nurse. But this time she simply couldn't handle it. Her stomach churned at the thought of it.

What is wrong with me? It's like I've become a full-blown wimp. These flu symptoms have been going on for too long.

Kelly stopped in front of the Band-Aids, bandages, medical tape, hydrocortisone cream, and more. How many days had she been suffering from the flu? *Okay, I was sick before our Valentine's date. . .actually, I was sick more than a week before that.*

She counted days on her fingers. "I've been fighting this for

133

well over two weeks." She took in a long, slow breath. "This is ridiculous. I haven't run a fever or had any chills. I'm just so nauseated and tired."

Kelly grabbed the cream and dropped it into the cart. She continued down the aisle in search of cotton balls. Her gaze took in the display of pregnancy tests. A weight dropped in her stomach. *No.* She shook her head. *No way. That's not possible. I had my tubes tied five years ago.*

She pulled her pocket calendar out of her purse. *Surely, it isn't possible.* She checked each month.

November?

Fine.

December?

Fine.

January?

She searched the days of January. No marks appeared before her eyes. No proof of the days she'd had her menstrual cycle. She flipped the calendar back to December, then counted the weeks to when she should have marked days in January.

She closed her eyes, trying to remember what she was doing on the days in question. Nothing was coming to mind. Why couldn't she remember having her cycle?

Opening her eyes slowly, she stared at the pregnancy tests before her. *I skipped my period.*

Glancing around her to be sure no one watched, Kelly grabbed a box and tucked it under other items in the cart. *I'm sure it's nothing, but if I go ahead and take the test it'll set my mind at ease.*

No longer able to finish her grocery shopping, Kelly sped toward the checkout line. *If I were pregnant, I would be far enough along that I wouldn't have to wait until morning to take the test. I could take it now.* The very thought weakened Kelly's knees. Her heart raced as she got in line behind an older man with a few items.

"Hey, Mrs. Smith. I can get you over here."

Kelly looked up and saw one of her junior students motion her to his line. Empty line.

Kelly's heart plummeted. She glanced around to see if there was anyone—anyone—within the vicinity who could jump into his line. No one. She looked at the older man in front of her who had started talking to the cashier and had yet to place the first item on the conveyor.

"Come on, Mrs. Smith." She glanced at her student, Jerome. He motioned at her again.

Her feet felt as heavy as bricks as she slowly scooted toward his line, begging God to send someone to jump in front of her. What would he think when he saw the pregnancy test? *Oh, Lord, what do I do? Maybe, I should just take it back and. . . I know. . .*

She smiled at her student from her third period class. "Hello, Jerome." She pointed to her cart. "I forgot to pick up some toothpaste. Maybe I'll catch you in a minute." She maneuvered the cart around and headed back toward hygiene products.

There. I didn't lie. We do need toothpaste. I'll pick some up. Then I'll just wait until his lane is full, and then I'll get in someone else's line.

Kelly grabbed a tube of toothpaste, dumped it into the cart, and then watched the checkout lanes. In only a matter of moments, a woman, probably the manager, had walked over to Jerome, pulled out his money, and closed his line. Breathing a sigh of relief, Kelly slipped into line behind a young woman and a toddler.

Kelly smiled at the little tike and waved her hand. He turned his face, as if bashful, then smiled one of the sweetest smiles she'd seen in a while. Soon enough, she'd have a grandchild making those adorable faces. *And maybe another child.*

Bile rose in her throat at the idea of it. *What woman had a child months after her grandchild was born?* The thought was ludicrous. Preposterous.

While his mother stood at the front of the cart fumbling through her purse, the little guy leaned over and grabbed a candy bar from the shelf. Before Kelly could respond, he shoved the wrapper into his mouth.

Kelly scrunched her nose. "That's yucky." She grabbed the wrapper from the child's hands, hoping it wasn't too germ-ridden. His lips puckered, and his face wrapped in the most wounded expression she'd ever seen. Wails, louder than tardy bell at school, expelled from the boy, and Kelly practically jumped out of her shoes.

"I'm sorry." She handed the candy bar to the child's mother, who now bore into Kelly with a menacing look. "He put this in his mouth. I'm sure it's not clean."

The woman didn't appear pleased with Kelly's decision to save the urchin from the threat of bacteria and virus as she took the candy bar from Kelly's grasp. She allowed the cashier to scan it, then pulled the chocolate from the wrapper and handed it to the boy. The child looked at Kelly as if she were the proverbial bully who'd taken away the child's sucker as he smashed the chocolate partly into his mouth, but mostly all over his face. Without a second glance, the woman finished paying and pushed the cart out of the aisle and toward the door.

The cashier, an older woman with white hair and a

quick smile, winked at Kelly. "That guy was too little to eat chocolate."

Kelly's chin quivered as she forced a smile. Usually not that emotional, Kelly focused on taking the items out of the cart. She tried not to look into the woman's kind eyes as she rang up each item.

"Hmm. This one doesn't want to scan."

Kelly glanced up and saw the woman holding the pregnancy test. She moved it across the laser once. Twice. Three times.

"Do you know how much this costs?" She held the box up in front of Kelly, and Kelly felt sure her legs were going to fall out from underneath her.

Kelly shook her head and opened her mouth to tell the woman not to worry about it. That she didn't need it.

The woman leaned into the microphone next to her cash register. "Price check on aisle 12. I need a price check, please."

Kelly felt heat flash up her neck and through her cheeks. "It's okay." She tried not to beg the woman. "I'll just get one later."

"Well, hey again, Mrs. Smith."

Kelly closed her eyes at the sound of Jerome's voice behind her. Taking in a deep breath, she turned and smiled at her student. "Hello, Jerome."

The cashier shoved the box into Jerome's hand. "I need you to go find out how much this pregnancy test costs."

Kelly gripped the cart with all her strength, praying her legs didn't give out from beneath her.

"No problem." Jerome waltzed toward the pharmacy section and returned within moments. He quoted the price and handed it back to the older woman. "See you Monday, Mrs. Smith."

Kelly nodded as she pulled her debit card from her purse. She paid the bill then took the receipt from the cashier. The woman winked again. "You'll be a wonderful mother."

Kelly couldn't respond. She raced to her car, loaded the bags, then sped to her house. Shoving the pregnancy test into the bottom of her purse, she took a deep breath then marched into the house.

"Mom, I—" said Brittany.

"Don't forget—" said Zoey.

Kelly stalked past them. "Sorry, girls. Gotta go to the bathroom first."

Shutting and locking the door, Kelly swallowed the knot in her throat. She tried not to think about Jerome and what he thought or what he'd say. She tried not to envision a litany of teenagers scoffing at the pregnancy of their "old" English teacher. The one whose teen daughter was also pregnant. She dug into the bottom of her purse and pulled out the box. With trembling fingers, she opened the test and read the instructions. "Times have changed," Kelly mumbled, "I don't have to wait until the morning anyway."

After getting the test ready, she closed her eyes. "God. . ." What did she say to Him? She was too old to have another baby. Thirty-eight, for goodness' sake. She was going to be a grandma. And yet she was still a woman. And there was still this small, slight, microscopic piece of her that wanted for the result to be positive. To see what Harold's child would look like. To cuddle her own newborn once more.

"God," she started again. "You know."

She took the test. Staring at the result, tears welled in her eyes. How can a woman feel happy and sad, scared and excited? She gripped the side of the bathroom sink. Staring at her reflection, that of a thirty-eight-year-old mother of three daughters and soon-to-be grandma, her heart raced as if it were about to explode. "I'm pregnant."

❧

After pushing the front door open, Harold tucked the dozen long-stemmed, red roses behind his back. He and Kelly hadn't been able to make up their Valentine's date, and though they'd spend this evening at Brittany's basketball game, he still wanted Kelly to know he longed for alone time with her. His bride of two months stood at the kitchen sink, her back to him. He sneaked up behind her and wrapped his free arm around her waist. She jumped and turned, but once recognition dawned in her gaze, Harold pressed his lips against hers.

"Harold," she whispered into his lips, and Harold longed to pull her closer.

Instead, he revealed the roses and handed them to Kelly. "We were never able to celebrate Valentine's Day properly." He kissed her forehead. "I love you, Kelly."

Kelly took the flowers from his hands and stared at them. Tears pooled in her eyes, and Harold brushed them away with his fingertips. She gazed up at him, and Harold expected her to thank him for the flowers, to declare she loved them, that he was wonderful for remembering red roses were her favorite. Instead, sadness lingered in her gaze. She seemed to hide herself behind a new wall that she built between them. But for what reason now?

They seemed to be settling into a routine as a family. Zoey, though still a pregnant teenager, had recommitted herself to God and seemed to be handling things well. Brittany and Candy thrived in school and in their activities. He couldn't think of a single reason for Kelly to shut him out. *Unless she just wishes she hadn't married me to begin with.*

He shook his head. He wouldn't allow his thoughts to go there. Quite frankly, it didn't matter if she did feel that way. He'd made a commitment before God, family, and friends. He vowed to love, honor, and cherish her in the good times and in the bad times, for better or for worse, and she'd simply have to learn to love him again. No turning back. The two were one flesh.

Unable to get a good grip on the frustration he felt, Harold strode down the hall. He looked in Candy's room. "Are you going to Brittany's game tonight?"

Candy looked up at him and frowned. He knew his tone was too terse. She hadn't done anything to upset him. "No. I have a project due tomorrow. I'm staying home with Zoey."

Harold should have asked her about it, but he still felt such aggravation toward Kelly that he simply nodded and made his way to Brittany's room. He knocked on the door. "It's time to go."

"Okay. I'll grab my stuff. You get Mom."

He strode into their bedroom and saw Kelly sitting on the bed. Red rims circled her eyes. "Harold. . ."

Harold didn't want to hear. He was tired of all the emotions, of all the crying and whimpering. Things didn't have to be as hard as his four women were always making them. He'd brought Kelly flowers. She had no reason to cry and shut him out. And he'd had enough of it. He pulled a few tissues out of the box and tossed them to Kelly. "Here." His voice was tense, angry, but he couldn't help it. "Clean up. We've got to go."

Without a backward glance, he stalked out to the car. In his anger, he'd forgotten his coat. He didn't need it. Frustration warmed him to his core. He started the car and waited for Kelly and Brittany to join him. Soon, they slipped into the car. The ride to the game was silent. Brittany seldom talked before she played, and Harold couldn't think of anything he could say to Kelly that would be in any way kind. Obviously, Kelly felt the same way.

Once at the game, Harold followed Kelly into the gym. They sat in their usual spot, midway up the stands on the right side. Harold smiled and nodded at the usual parents who joined them in their normal places as well. Within moments, the girls' team had emerged from the locker room to the shouts and cheers of the hometown fans.

Determined not to think about Kelly, Harold watched Brittany as she warmed up with her team. He felt such pride when his stepdaughter dribbled the ball from one hand to the other with ease. It was something she and he had practiced multiple times over in the driveway the past summer. Kelly's girls had become like his own children; he could only imagine how much more pride the biological dads of these girls felt.

"Hi, Ms. Smith," said a tall, African American boy scaling the steps beside them.

Harold looked at Kelly. Her face turned bright crimson as she merely nodded then peered down at her feet. Harold furrowed his eyebrows. *That's not like Kelly.* Normally, she smiles, waves, even strikes up conversations with her students. She'd always been the friendliest teacher he'd ever seen when she saw her students in public settings.

Maybe that kid's a troublemaker. Harold glanced up the stands at the boy. The guy looked familiar. If Harold's guess was right, he was the one who worked at their local grocery store. Harold studied the boy a moment longer. *Yeah. That's definitely the kid from the grocery. He's a great kid. Why would Kelly act so funny with him?*

Harold peered at his wife. Desperation traced her features. He couldn't fathom what was wrong with her. He touched her leg. She jumped. He frowned. "Kelly, what is wrong?"

"Nothing." The word came out loud and a note higher than she usually talked. "I've just got to go to the bathroom." She stood, and Harold watched as she walked down the steps then out of the gym.

Harold sighed. *God, I have no idea what is going on with her.* He propped his feet on the row in front him then leaned forward resting his elbows on his knees. He rested his chin on his fists. *I'm just going to focus on the game.*

He gazed up at the scoreboard. The game would start in less than two minutes. Brittany and her team had huddled around their coach by the bench. Harold couldn't help but chuckle at how much taller Brittany, a freshman, was than the rest of her teammates. Though still one of the weaker players, due to being thin and not fully matured, Brittany started as the center for the team. Brittany's dribbling skills warranted her a position as a guard, but the team's desperate need for a strong center won out, and Harold found himself trying to help his fifteen-year-old stepdaughter beef up in weight and strength.

With only seconds left on the clock before the game started, Kelly made her way back up the steps and sat beside Harold. Too frustrated to talk to her, Harold didn't ask if everything was all right. She wouldn't have told him anyway. The woman had spent more time shutting him out in the two months of their marriage than she'd spent opening up to him in the year they dated. This should be the most exciting time of their marriage, and yet Harold found himself growing more confused and flustered by his new wife.

Harold clapped while the other team was announced and stood and cheered when it was Brittany's team's turn. The teams lined up on the floor, and Harold howled when Brittany got the tip-off. He watched the game intently, no longer thinking about Kelly and her odd reactions of late.

"Hi, Mrs. Smith."

Harold looked over at the aisle. Two girls stood beside Kelly. The one talking smiled like a Cheshire cat. "Jerome told us he saw you at the grocery."

Kelly's face blanched, and she shifted in her seat. "Hello, girls." Kelly gripped her purse strap and twisted it. "I see Jerome at the store all the time."

Jerome. That's the boy's name from the store. Kelly's apprehension at talking to the girls stumped Harold. He peered back up the stands at the African American boy who'd spoken to Kelly earlier. He was standing, crossing his hand in front of him and shaking his head. He mouthed the word "no" repeatedly, and if Harold guessed right, it appeared Jerome was looking at the two girls talking to Kelly. Harold looked back at his wife.

"Yeah, but this was a couple of days ago." The girl's expression was arrogant and a bit bratty. "He said he had to help you with a price check."

The blond beside the girl giggled then shifted next to her friend.

"Jerome helps with price checks all the time." Kelly's voice had a fearful lilt to it. It almost sounded like panic.

"Yeah, but what did Mr. Smith think about this price check?"

The girl's tone was sarcastic and disrespectful, and Harold opened his mouth to tell her that it was time for her to go on back to her seat, when Kelly jumped up. "Excuse me, girls."

She pushed past the girls, nearly raced down the steps, and out of the gym door.

The girl looked at Harold and huffed. "I take it that means you don't know about her price check." The girl turned to her friend and shrugged. The blond giggled again and tugged on the mouthy girl to head back up the steps. He heard her mumble to her friend. "Poor guy."

Harold frowned. *What could possibly be going on with Kelly and some price check? And why would she let that teenage girl talk to her in such a disrespectful way?* In all the time he'd known Kelly he'd never seen her show a moment of weakness in front of one of her students, but tonight she practically ran out the door.

Harold looked up at the teenage girl. He had half a mind to stomp up those steps and tell that child she needed to find her teacher and apologize. He took a long breath. The girl didn't know him. He didn't know her. Kelly shouldn't have let her talk like that. It was almost as if she had something to hide from him. *But why is she always trying to hide things from me, God?*

Frustrated, Harold peered back down at the basketball court. He'd missed the last three baskets. He hadn't even heard the announcer say who'd made the shots. His phone buzzed. He pulled it out of his pocket and opened the text. It was from Kelly. She was going to stay in the car the rest of the game. She doesn't feel well, Harold grumbled at the last bit of her message.

Tonight, he was tired of her being sick. He was finished

with her being secretive and trying to shut him out of her life. Tonight, he was going to watch his stepdaughter play basketball. *If Kelly won't let me in on what's going on, she can just wait in the car.*

He clapped as the buzzer sounded signifying the end of the first quarter. "God, I never thought I'd be saying this only two months in, but please, help my marriage."

thirteen

It was Monday, and Kelly still hadn't started her cycle, she'd taken two more pregnancy tests, and they still came back positive. *Thank You, Lord, that I won't have to face my students today, since they're out of school and we have professional development.* But then, Kelly would be missing that, as well. She'd have to make up the hours at a later date. Today, she was going to Zoey's ultrasound appointment. She peered at her reflection in the mirror and mumbled, "It's going to be a great day. I get to find out the sex of my grandchild and if they're doing okay." She clasped her hands in front of her chest. "And I get to make an appointment to find out about my baby."

Her expression sombered, and she plopped onto the toilet cover. "And I need to tell Harold."

Her stomach groaned with anxiety at the thought of what he would say. She'd had her tubes tied five years before, she never even considered worrying about getting pregnant. Besides, she was thirty-eight years old, not that she was too old, but when she was the mother of teenagers and about to be a grandmother—Kelly shook her head and sighed. This whole situation was ridiculously overwhelming.

She remembered the way he'd laughed when Sadie had mistakenly guessed that she and Harold were pregnant. He made it abundantly obvious that the last thing he wanted was for the two of them to have a child.

A knock sounded on the bathroom door. "Come on, Kelly.

We don't want to be late."

Kelly groaned. And Harold was going with them to the appointment. Ever since he'd taken Zoey shopping for maternity clothes, Zoey wanted Harold to be a part of everything. Kelly couldn't believe he'd agreed to take the morning off to go to the ultrasound with them. Of course, she'd seen the look of shock and uncertainty that wrapped Harold's features when Zoey asked him to go. It was apparent he didn't feel exceptionally comfortable with the idea. But she also knew that Harold wouldn't say no.

It was one of the things she loved about him.

What's he going to say when he finds out he and I are going to have a baby? We'll be raising our child and grandchild at the same time, as if they were cousins. The very idea. . . Kelly stood and walked out of the bathroom. *Just don't think about it right now. One thing at a time.*

"Come on, Mom," Zoey hollered from the front of the house.

"I'm coming." Kelly opened Candy's door. Her youngest was still fast asleep, swaddled in a pile of covers. She gently shut the door, then headed toward Brittany's room. Kelly could barely get the door open from the clutter on the floor. *This kid's going to clean her room today.* She peered in at Brittany. She was asleep, as well. They'd probably be home before either girl awakened. Kelly shut the door, grabbed her coat, and slipped it on. She picked up her purse from the table and shut and locked the door.

As she walked down the sidewalk toward the car, she looked at Harold. His discomfort at going to Zoey's ultrasound was obvious, but she could tell he'd do whatever Zoey asked. She loved that about Harold. A vision of his expression when she told him she, too, was pregnant flashed through her mind. It wasn't pretty. She pushed it away. She could only imagine what he would think.

&

Harold wanted to crawl out of the doctor's room when Zoey lay on the bed and the nurse prepared her for the ultrasound. Standing close to Zoey's head, he focused on the blank screen that would soon show Zoey's baby. *Why in the world would she want me here?* Harold forced himself not to cringe. He couldn't recall a time he'd felt more uncomfortable.

But Zoey had changed so much since she'd recommitted herself to the Lord. He caught her reading her Bible all the time. She journaled constantly, and though he'd never read anything she wrote, he had a feeling she was often talking to God because her Bible always lay on top of her journal.

She also sought Harold out every day to talk to him about one thing or another. It had even been her idea for him to take her and her sisters to a movie the following weekend. *"It'll be a father/daughter date."* Her words ran through his mind. He'd nearly swallowed his tongue when she said that. He wanted so much for the girls to think of him as a father. Having never had children and knowing he never would, Harold found himself enjoying being a father to Kelly's girls.

"Okay, we're ready." The nurse's voice shook Harold from his thoughts.

He peered in amazement as the figure of a baby formed on the screen. The picture was so clear, so precise, it was almost like looking at a black-and-white photo of the child. The woman marked and clicked at various places, confirming the heart, the spine, the legs, that everything appeared as it should.

"Would you like to know the sex of the baby?" the nurse asked.

"Yes," Harold replied. His cheeks warmed as Kelly and Zoey chuckled at his excitement. He looked at their faces. "I mean, if you all want to."

"Sure," Zoey said.

"He's a boy," the nurse said.

A boy. Harold would have a blast playing with the little guy. He patted Zoey's shoulder. "He looks pretty strong."

Zoey chuckled. "Could I get two copies of the pictures you've taken? Someone else would like copies."

Harold frowned. *Had Jamie come back to town? Was she seeing him and they didn't know it?* His heart raced at the thought. Christian or not, Harold wasn't sure how he would respond if he ever saw Jamie again. The man had taken advantage of Zoey, and Harold wasn't sure he would be able to control his temper if he saw the guy.

Harold's thoughts must have gotten away from him because when he looked back at Zoey, the nurse had already left and Zoey was sitting on the edge of the patient bed. She gripped the photos in her hands. "I need to talk to you both."

Her tone was serious, and Harold looked from Zoey to Kelly. His wife hadn't said two words since they'd gotten to the doctor's office. She'd spoken with the receptionist for several minutes when they'd first arrived, but since then she'd been completely silent. Even throughout the entire ultrasound.

"I was going to wait until we got home." Zoey peered down at the pictures. "But I think I'll go ahead and tell you now."

If she said she was going to run off with that low-down, no-good fellow who got her pregnant Harold wouldn't be responsible for his actions. *God, I know we're supposed to love everyone. We're supposed to forgive. But if Zoey is so foolish as to think that man would do right by her. . .* Harold's blood boiled. His heart nearly beat out of his chest. His fists balled, and he knew that if it was within his power, no man would hurt his little girl.

And she was his little girl now.

He looked at his wife, whose face had blanched. Her hand rested at the nape of her neck. It trembled ever so slightly, and Harold knew she had no idea what Zoey was going to say. Though Kelly was as beautiful as ever, the last few months had taken a toll on her. Dark lines rested beneath her eyes, and Harold knew she hadn't slept well in a long while. She'd barely talked to him since the game on Friday night, and Harold had no idea what to do with her.

Just love her. That's all I can do.

"I've made a decision."

Harold looked back at Zoey. She peered up at her mother, then toward Harold. "I've been praying about it. Really seeking God's will. I've messed up, but God has forgiven me and now I want to live for Him, to do what He wills."

Harold swallowed. His stepdaughter sounded so serious, so old. He believed that she'd sought God on whatever she was about to tell them. He'd watched her, and he knew she'd changed. He gazed at Kelly. She sat back down in the chair beside Zoey.

"What is it, Zoey?" Kelly's voice sounded tired.

"And I've already talked with Cam and Sadie about it. I think it's for the best."

Cam and Sadie? What did they have to do with any of this?

Zoey held up the pictures of her little boy. "I've decided to allow Cam and Sadie to adopt my son."

Harold let out a breath he hadn't realized he'd been holding in. The idea bounced back and forth through his mind. Cam and Sadie were wonderful parents, and they would adore Zoey's child. The more he thought about it, the more Harold realized the idea was a good one.

"I'm not ready to be a mom." Zoey looked at her mother. "Cam and Sadie could give my son everything he needed, and he'd have a big sister. And I would still be able to see him. . ."

"I don't know if you realize how hard giving up your baby would be." Kelly's tone was low and serious, her expression blank.

"You're right, Mom. I don't, but I love him enough to do what's right for him. I'll barely be eighteen when he's born."

"I was twenty when I had you."

Harold frowned. Allowing Cam and Sadie to adopt the child seemed to be the perfect solution. Zoey could go on to college. She could still see her son on a regular basis. And Kelly knew she'd been seeking God's will for her life. He frowned at Kelly. "It sounds like she's prayed a lot about this, Kelly."

Kelly stared up at Harold. "I'm not saying she shouldn't give her son up for adoption." She looked back at Zoey. "I just want to be sure she understands that either way, having a baby is a life-changing experience. Once you've become pregnant, there's no going back." She looked back up at Harold, and he wondered at the pleading expression on her face. "A pregnancy changes everything."

Zoey grabbed Kelly's hand. "I believe you, Mom. I feel this is what God wants. Will you pray with me about it?"

Kelly wrapped her arms around her daughter. "Of course I will."

Harold felt perplexed at Kelly's response. What was going on with his wife?

❧

Kelly was thankful that for the last few days she hadn't felt quite as nauseated. She followed Harold and Zoey into the house. They'd just left Zoey's ultrasound appointment. Zoey and Harold had talked nonstop about her notion of giving Kelly's grandchild to Cam and Sadie. In the depths of Kelly's spirit, she knew Zoey was making the right choice. She'd support her daughter completely.

At the same time, it broke Kelly's heart to know that Zoey would experience heartache and trials no matter what she chose. Being a young mother herself when she had Zoey, she knew how overwhelming the physical care for a new baby would be. Kelly'd had the support of a loving husband when she'd had Zoey. But Kelly also knew that giving away a child would be equally as difficult. How many times had she and Sadie talked about Sadie's longings to be Ellie's mother? How would Zoey respond when her son called Sadie "Mom" or when Cam and Sadie had to discipline him or when he ran to them for help with a boo-boo. Either way, Zoey would experience pain and loss, and it broke Kelly's heart that her daughter would go through that.

"Hi, Mom," Candy squealed as they walked through the door. "Hey, Harold." She wrapped her arms around Harold in a hug.

"So, what's Zoey having?" Brittany asked.

"A boy," Zoey responded. "But I'm giving him up for adoption."

"You're what?" Candy's voice raised two octaves and she peered at her oldest sister.

"To Cam and Sadie," Zoey said seriously.

"Mom, did you know this?" Shock wrapped Brittany's expression.

Kelly couldn't handle this right now. She waved her hand. "Let me go to the bathroom, then we'll all talk."

Kelly practically raced past her daughters and into her bathroom. She shut the door, allowing her whole body to lean against it. She could hear Zoey and Harold talking to the girls about the baby. It was evident Harold supported Zoey's decision completely.

She couldn't blame him. The man was forty years old. He didn't have any siblings. He'd been thrown into a marriage of a bunch of nutty, hormonal women and learned on his honeymoon that his teenage stepdaughter was going to have a baby. He didn't want a baby in the house. His response had been overwhelmingly obvious of the fact.

Adoption to Cam and Sadie probably is the best thing for Zoey's baby, her spirit nudged her.

And Harold had never given Kelly any reason to think he wouldn't have been willing to keep Zoey's baby.

Being willing and wanting a child are two different things.

She growled as she flopped on the toilet cover. *I started my day worrying right here.*

She shook her head. Harold was going to completely freak out when he found out she was pregnant. She pulled her doctor's appointment slip from her purse. Because of her age and the fact that she'd had her tubes tied, the receptionist had made an appointment for her to see the doctor the following week.

One week. She would love to wait until after her appointment to tell Harold about the pregnancy, but she thought of the students from school. By tomorrow morning, Brittany would probably hear rumors that her mom had bought a pregnancy test.

No. She couldn't wait the seven days. She'd have to tell Harold. She'd have to tell him tonight. The thought made Kelly's stomach churn. Her heart raced, her palms grew sweaty. *How much could one man take?* They hadn't even been married three months. The poor guy would probably go running and screaming from the house, vowing never to return.

A mental image filled her mind of her oversized, dark-haired husband flailing his arms through the air and racing from the house. She could see him in his light brown work shirt and stained darker brown pants. His big, clunky boots would leave massive prints in the snow. A smile bowed her lips. The image was too funny, and it lightened her mood.

God, You already know everything.

She shoved the appointment slip back into her purse and shrugged her shoulders. The truth was she was the mother of a seventeen-year-old pregnant daughter. She had a fifteen-year-old daughter who was a living, breathing, walking tornado, leaving traces of food, clothes, and dirt everywhere she went. She was the mother of an eleven-year-old whose body was beginning to blossom and who begged almost every day to shave her legs, wear makeup, and get a cell phone. And now, she was pregnant with her new husband's baby.

She lived a wacky life. It was the one God had given her. She was nervous about Harold's response, however she had no choice but to tell him. In the meantime, she'd change her attitude. *God, my life belongs to You. And if another baby is what You want. . .*

She shrugged her shoulders and opened the bathroom door.

She could hear the girls talking over each other, and Harold's intermittent attempt to get in a word of his own. She sighed. *Then a baby is what we'll have.*

fourteen

Harold settled into bed. It had been a long day. He'd intended to go in to work after Zoey's ultrasound appointment, but when Zoey announced she'd be giving the baby to Cam and Sadie, his girls had needed him. They'd all done a lot of talking and praying. Thankfully, when he'd called Rudy to see how things were going at work, Rudy told him he and Walt had everything covered. *I'll just go in a bit earlier tomorrow.*

He turned toward his alarm clock and reset it for four thirty. After picking up his Bible, he turned to the book of Acts. He'd been reading through his Bible one chapter a night for several years. As much as he hated reading, he found his relationship with the Lord deepened just by reading a bit of Scripture each night. *Even I can handle one chapter per night.*

Kelly walked out of the bathroom. She wore a long flannel nightgown that practically covered every inch of her body from her neck all the way down her arms and all the way down to her ankles. She padded on bare feet to the dresser, where she opened the top drawer, pulled out a pair of fluffy red socks, and quickly shoved them on her feet. He couldn't help but chuckle.

Kelly looked at him. Her face had been newly cleaned and was shiny from whatever lotion or cream she put on each night. She'd put some kind of band around her head to keep any hair from touching her face. "You know I freeze at night."

Harold patted the bed. "I think you look adorable."

She slipped into bed beside him and reached for a bottle

of lotion on her end table. While she rubbed the flowery smelling stuff on her hands, Harold looked back at his Bible and started to read.

"Harold," Kelly whispered. "Do you love me?"

"You know I do," Harold mumbled and continued to focus on the words in front of him. He read about the Lord telling Ananias to go to Straight Street to look for a man named Saul. God's precise instructions always fascinated him. The Lord was specific, and Harold loved that about Him.

"Harold," Kelly whispered again. "You know I love you, too."

"Mmmhmm." Harold continued to read about Ananias's fear about the harm Saul had already done to the Christians. Harold wondered if he would voice his concern to God as Ananias did. If Harold heard God's audible voice, he hoped he'd respond affirmatively right away. *But then sometimes I realize later He's right next to me trying to tell me something important, but I'm oblivious to His voice.*

"Harold," Kelly whispered again. "How much do you love me?"

"A whole bunch," Harold mumbled, as he continued to read the Lord's emphatic instruction to Ananias to do as God said. Ananias needed to listen to God and not doubt the men He chose to spread His word. *Lord, I just don't think I would be so hardheaded. I think I would recognize that I needed to listen to You, to heed what You said.*

"Harold. . ."

"Hmm?" Harold continued to read. When Ananias placed his hands on Saul and spoke to him, scales fell from Saul's eyes. He immediately got up and was baptized. Saul didn't waste any time acknowledging God's prodding. *Well, he did spend three days blind, though, didn't he?*

"What if things changed?"

Harold looked at Kelly for the first time. What had she been talking to him about? He was trying to read his Bible, trying to unwind from a long day. What was all this concern about him loving her and her loving him? She knew he loved her. She'd been the one going bonkers on him lately. "What are you talking about, Kelly?"

She twisted a bit of the gown between her hands. "I just need to know that you love me."

"Of course I love you."

"No matter what."

He touched her chin. "No matter what." He looked back at his Bible.

"Even if things changed."

Harold looked at Kelly and frowned. "Can things change any more then they already have?"

She nodded. Fear traced her features. Maybe it wasn't fear, but more like hesitancy. But what could she be hesitant to tell him? He didn't believe there was a thing in the world Kelly could say that would surprise him. "When you married into my family, I should have warned you that things could always change—a lot."

He took her hands into his. "Not my love for you."

"That's good. . ." Kelly hesitated. She shut her mouth, then opened it again. " 'Cause. . ." She let out a long breath.

Concern worked its way through Harold's veins. What would Kelly possibly have to tell him that had her so nervous to just come out and say it? "Kelly?"

She pulled her hands away from his and covered her eyes. "I'm pregnant."

Harold stared at her. The words played once, twice, then a third time through his mind. "Did you say. . . ?"

She lowered her hands and pouted. "I said I'm pregnant."

"You're pregnant?" Harold felt his eyebrows raise, felt his mouth gape open. Excitement coursed through his body. He would be a father, a biological father, a father to a baby, then a kid, then a teenager. He'd get to go through all the steps and not just take the kid on once he'd gotten too smart for his own good. "You're pregnant!"

"I'm sorry." Kelly frowned and the pout deepened. "I never dreamed we'd have to take precautions. My tubes were tied, and I just can't—I can't believe it."

"You're pregnant!" Harold couldn't stop saying it. He was going to be a daddy. He was going to hold his own son in his arms. They would play catch together, go fishing together, and do all the things dads and sons did together. Never in his wildest imaginations did he ever dream he'd have the opportunity to have his own child. *God, what a blessing! What an unbelievable blessing!*

Harold pulled Kelly over to him, wrapping his arms around her. "Oh, Kelly."

"I'm sorry, Harold."

"Sorry?" Harold raked his fingers through her hair. "I can't remember the last time I've been so excited." He released her long enough to cup her cheeks in his hands. "I never thought I'd have my own child." He pressed his lips against hers. "You've given me the best gift."

"You're happy?" Kelly's voice sounded surprised.

Harold jumped out of bed. "I'm more than happy. Girls!" he yelled. "Girls!"

Candy raced into the room. "What?" Brittany and Zoey followed behind her.

"Harold!" Kelly said. "I didn't expect you to tell them so quickly."

"Why not? It's the most wonderful news in the world." He turned toward his stepdaughters. "Your mom is pregnant."

৵

Harold's response had not been what she expected. But his excitement had eased her concerns and allowed her to consider what it would be like to have a baby in the home again—one that she and her husband would raise as their own child.

Candy and Brittany had been overjoyed, every bit as excited as Harold. Zoey had been more reserved. Kelly admitted the idea of the two of them being pregnant together seemed odd to her, as well. *Definitely isn't something I ever intended to happen.*

The next morning as she drove to the high school, Kelly thought about Harold placing his hands on her still somewhat flat stomach. He'd kissed her beside her belly button. "Good morning, baby." He patted her stomach, then stood and kissed her lips. "Eat right today. Make sure you don't let your students stress you out. Sit down every chance you can."

Kelly laughed at the memory. Harold would probably drive her crazy for the next several months. Her cell phone rang, and Kelly pulled it out of her purse and answered it. "Hello."

"Hey, Kelly." Sadie's voice sounded over the line. "I hear you have some big news."

"I'm guessing Zoey called you." Kelly couldn't help smiling into the phone. Sadie had been a terrific sister-in-law, and Kelly knew she'd been an encouragement to Zoey through the last several months.

"She did."

"Is she upset about me being pregnant, too?" Just saying the words aloud caused Kelly to scrunch her nose. She was relieved with Harold's excitement at the pregnancy, and she'd begun to allow herself to wrap her mind around being a mother of a newborn again, but it was still strange to be pregnant the same time as her daughter.

"Not upset," Sadie said. "Just a little weirded out."

Kelly laughed. "I'm a little weirded out, too."

"How do you feel about her news? About adoption, I mean."

"I was surprised, and I'm not at all opposed to it. I guess I just hadn't considered—"

"I just want you to know I never mentioned it to her. She came to Cam and me and asked us if we'd be willing to adopt the baby. We prayed about it for a while before we agreed. I don't want you to think—"

"You were trying to steal my grandbaby." Kelly laughed. "I know that, Sadie. In my heart, I know you and Cam are the best parents for her baby. It just hurts me that she's going to hurt. If she keeps the baby, she'll hurt. If she gives the baby to you, she'll hurt."

"You're absolutely right."

Kelly pulled into the school's parking lot. "Listen, I just pulled into work. I'll talk to you later, okay?"

"Okay."

Kelly clicked her phone off, grabbed her purse and lunch, and walked into the school. She opened her classroom, walked inside, and turned on her computer. Several messages showed in her inbox. She clicked the first one. It was one of her fellow language arts teachers asking her if she was pregnant. The next was from the curriculum teacher asking if there was anything she could do to help Kelly. Kelly didn't click the next. She shook her head. *Boy, word sure travels fast. It's a good thing I talked to Harold last night. And I'm glad he went ahead and told the girls.*

Kelly walked to the whiteboard and wrote her bell ringer for the day. Ironically, her junior class students were reading *The Scarlet Letter*. Though there was no sin involved in Kelly being pregnant, it still felt a little weird for her and her daughter to be pregnant at the same time. And Kelly still felt a little old.

The bell rang, and Kelly mentally prepared herself for the questions that were sure to come from student after student as the day progressed. She walked to her desk to be sure her worksheets were ready for the day. As expected, Logan was the first student in the room.

"Hey, Mrs. Smith." Logan dropped his books on the desk and walked toward Kelly.

"Hi, Logan. How was your three-day weekend?"

"It was good. My parents made us drive to Pennsylvania to visit my grandparents. Kind of boring, but it was okay."

"That's good." Kelly arranged the worksheets on her desk in order that she would need them.

"Can I ask you a question, Mrs. Smith?"

Oh boy, here it comes. "Sure. Go ahead."

"I heard you're pregnant. Is that true?"

Kelly let out a long breath. "Yep. It's true."

"Cool." Logan nodded. "My mom's having a baby next month."

"Really?" Kelly peered at Logan. "How old is your mother?" She shook her head. "I mean, it doesn't matter. . . ."

"It's okay. My mom's forty-three. She said the little guy was a bit of a surprise."

"Oh." Kelly's mind raced. She felt so old, so awkward having a baby at thirty-eight. Of course, Logan's mom wasn't having a baby the same time as her daughter.

"Yeah. It was a little weird because my older brother's already married with a kid. So his kid will be older than her uncle."

"Really?" Kelly drank in the information. Maybe she and Zoey weren't such an anomaly after all. The second bell rang and Kelly motioned toward Logan's seat. "It was nice talking to you, Logan, but we better start class."

Kelly walked toward the front of the room. *Thanks for that, God. I needed to know that someone else is going through close to the same thing as me.* She looked at her class, stopping at Logan. *Maybe I should call Logan's mom today, and tell her how much I enjoy having him in class.*

ža

Harold could hardly wait for the nurse to call them back to the room. He gripped Kelly's hand in his. He couldn't wait to find out her due date. Kelly said they might even be able to hear the baby's heartbeat. Harold had never heard a baby's heartbeat—well, except Zoey's baby, but this would be his baby.

He couldn't believe the emotions he felt over Kelly's pregnancy. He wanted to protect her, to make sure she ate properly, rested properly. He didn't want her to clean the bathrooms for fear the fumes would be too strong. Brittany had complained awhile about it, but he'd held firm that she, he, and Candy would take turns cleaning the bathrooms.

A young, light-haired woman opened the door leading to the examining rooms. "Kelly Smith."

Harold jumped up. He turned to Kelly, grabbed her hand, and helped her up. "Come on, hun."

Kelly giggled. "Harold, you're silly."

He nudged her forward, and they followed the woman back to the room where Zoey had her ultrasound. "I don't know if

Marge called and told you, but the doctor wants you to have an ultrasound before he sees you." She looked at Kelly's chart. "It says here you had your tubes tied five years ago."

Kelly nodded, and Harold could feel she'd become nervous. Harold had no idea that an ultrasound would be a bad thing. *God, please let our baby be okay.*

The woman smiled. "Don't worry. It's just a precaution." She handed Kelly a half paper, half tissue blanket. "Go ahead and undress from the waist down. The ultrasound technician will be back in a minute."

Harold sat in an empty chair, while Kelly slipped out of her skirt and placed the blanket over her waist. He studied his wife. "Do you feel okay?"

"Yes, Harold. I'm sure everything is fine."

He could tell by the lilt in her voice that she was nervous. "You've never had an ultrasound this early before, have you?"

She shook her head.

Harold moved his chair closer to her. "Talk to me, Kelly. Be honest with me. You're scared."

She sighed. "I am scared. I'm older. I'm more tired than I've ever been."

"Is that normal?"

Kelly shrugged. "I don't know. Probably."

The nurse-technician-whatever she was called walked into the room. "Hello, Mr. and Mrs. Smith. How's Zoey doing?"

"Fine." Kelly's voice sounded weak. "It's a little funny to have me in here now, huh?"

"Don't worry about that." The woman patted Kelly's leg. "Babies are blessings."

Harold listened as the woman explained this ultrasound would be different than Zoey's because Kelly was so early in the pregnancy, but she assured them everything would be all right. Harold watched his wife for any signs of pain, but she seemed fine and he simply squeezed her hand to show her that he was supporting her.

Once again, the blank screen came alive with various shades of blacks and grays. Their baby didn't look the same as Zoey's had. Zoey's baby looked like a real baby, one a guy could hold. His baby's head was a lot bigger than the rest of his body. His arms and legs were there, but they seemed so scrawny.

Just as she had with Zoey, the technician clicked several places of the baby's image, measuring the head, the arms, the legs.

"Well, what do we have here?" the woman said.

"What?" Harold leaned closer to the screen. He couldn't see anything. He didn't know what he was looking for. He glanced at Kelly. She appeared confused and worried. He gently kissed her forehead.

"Hang on. Just a sec."

The woman moved the ultrasound instrument a little bit, and Kelly winced.

"What are you doing?" Harold demanded. He knew he sounded fiercer then he should, but the woman needed to spit out what was going on.

"Hang on." She touched Kelly's leg. "I know this is a bit uncomfortable, but I think—yep, there it is." She pointed to the screen. "Looky there."

"What?" Harold peered at the screen. He didn't know what he was looking at. Another round circle in Kelly's stomach. What was that? What was wrong?

Kelly gasped. "You're kidding."

The technician giggled. "Not kidding, Mrs. Smith. Do you know what that is?"

"What?" Harold wanted to scream at the two of them. What was wrong with his wife?

"Harold." Kelly grabbed his jaw and tugged at his face until he gazed into her eyes. Tears pooled in them once again, and Harold felt mad with anxiety.

"What is it, Kelly?"

"We're having twins."

"Twins!" Harold jumped out of his seat. "Two babies."

The technician looked at the screen. She started pushing buttons again, measuring the head, arms, and legs of his second child.

"Kelly!" Harold leaned over and kissed her forehead. "Two babies."

Tears streamed down her cheeks. "Harold, what will we do with two babies?" This time it wasn't fear that sounded in her voice. A slight giggle sounded behind her words.

"We're going to love them." Harold pumped his fist. "I'm having two babies. Two boys."

"Or girls," Kelly said.

Harold leaned toward the screen again. "Can you tell that yet?"

The technician laughed. "Not yet."

Harold gazed back at his wife. "Two babies, Kelly! We're having two babies!" He kissed her forehead, her nose, then finally her lips.

"Ahem." The technician cleared her throat.

Harold looked over at her, and the woman smiled. He gazed back at Kelly. "You've made me the happiest man alive."

Kelly laughed. "You say that until we're waist high in stinky diapers and dirty bottles."

"I'll say it then, too. I love you, Kelly Smith."

"I love you, too, Harold."

epilogue

Kelly gazed around the room at the collection of family members who'd come to celebrate her day. It was like déjà vu. Her parents, in their midsixties, still looked young and lively—and very much in love. Her father gazed at his wife and winked as he ran his hand through his salt-and-pepper hair, his striking blue eyes sparkling. She gave him a sweet smile in return. Despite battling arthritis, Kelly's mother wore her hair and makeup with perfection, and the spry woman was still as stylish and trendy as a woman in her thirties.

One year ago Kelly wasn't even engaged to Harold. Now, she was married—she twisted in her seat—pregnant, and about to pop, and her grandson sat nestled in her daughter's lap. Though Cam and Sadie were little Micah's legal mom and dad, when they visited they always allowed Zoey to take care of him. Soon, Kelly's oldest daughter would be living in Wilmington and going to college there.

The babies within her womb seemed to fight more fervently for space, and Kelly was anxious for the month to pass so that she could nestle her new children.

Harold and the girls had finished the babies' room just a week before. He'd been so protective that the only thing he allowed Kelly to do was pick out a theme. He wouldn't let her paint, hang curtains, nothing. She got to watch. She didn't complain. Carrying twins at thirty-eight, now thirty-nine, had not been the same as carrying a single child at the ages of twenty, twenty-two, and twenty-six.

Harold walked out of the kitchen. He placed his hands over Kelly's belly. "How are my guys doing?"

Kelly chuckled. "You do realize they could be girls."

Harold shrugged. "Okay, or girls."

"Do you wish we'd found out the sex of the babies?"

Harold kissed the top of her head. "Nah. I don't care either way."

"Is that why you put up a train set in their room?"

"Girls can like trains, too."

Kelly shook her head. She shuffled in her seat again. "These kiddos are killing me today."

Concern traced Harold's features, and Kelly noted the light gray wisps of hair he'd gotten in the year since they married. "You need to lie down?"

"No, I'll be fine."

Before Harold could say anything else, Brittany and Candy walked out of the kitchen holding Kelly's cake. The entire top of the pastry seemed to be on fire, and Kelly wondered how a woman her age would ever keep up with two active babies. *I'll be leaning on You big-time, Lord.*

This year she'd had a lot of practice at putting her full faith in her heavenly Father. It had been a time fraught with trials of every kind. She looked around the room at the family God had given her. Her gaze rested on her sweet husband. God had also filled her life with more blessings then Kelly could count.

"Time to blow out your candles," Candy said.

Kelly pushed her way to a standing position. "Happy birthday to you. . ." echoed through her home, and Kelly sang along with the family. Once the song was finished, Kelly closed her eyes, made a wish, then blew out the candles.

She opened her eyes and grabbed the bottom of her belly. "Uh-oh."

Harold jumped up and grabbed her shoulders. "Kelly, what is it?"

"My water just broke."

≈

Harold stood at Kelly's side as the doctors performed the emergency C-section on his wife. Initially, they'd wanted him to stay out, but Harold wouldn't have any part in it, and when Kelly also voiced her desire for him to stay with her, the doctor had finally relented.

He kissed the top of Kelly's forehead. "It's going to be okay."

"It's too early."

"Only five weeks early." Harold tried to sound confident.

Tears streamed down Kelly's temples. She was so scared, more scared then he'd ever seen her. He wanted so much to take her fear away, to do whatever he had to do to make sure that Kelly was safe and felt secure. Right now, all he could do was whisper words of comfort in her ear.

"Pray for me," she whimpered.

"Okay." Harold gently rested his forehead against Kelly's. "Please, dear Jesus, wrap Your arms around Kelly. Give her peace. Let our babies be okay. Bring them into the world strong and healthy. Let them thrive. Help us be good parents to them. You have given them to us. Be with Kelly, Lord. I love her."

He lifted his head and kissed her forehead again. She whimpered slightly then murmured, "Thank you, Harold."

Harold kept his gaze focused on his wife. He was too nervous to look at the doctor and nurses. There were so many in the room. He didn't look up, but he could feel the people who stood beside tiny baby beds, ready to whisk his children away if necessary.

A moment passed and he heard a baby cry. Excited, he looked at the doctor. The tiny, red child squealed at the top of its lungs. "One girl."

Before Harold could fully focus or even respond, the doctor handed the child to a nurse, reached down, and pulled out his second child. This one was smaller, but the wails were just as strong. "A second girl," the doctor said.

Kelly's sobs of joy forced his attention back to her. He brushed her hair away from her face and looked back at his babies. "Kelly," he whispered against her ear.

Her laugh was hesitant and filled with emotion. "I told you we could have girls."

Worried for his wife, Harold stayed close to her side. He watched as the nurses wiped off his daughters, cleaned out their throats, and weighed them. He thought of flighty moods, the crazy hormones, the tantrums, the arguments, the hairspray and makeup, the outfit checks, and phone calls from boys. He thought of the gray hair that had formed since marrying Kelly. The proof that he loved and lived with a crew of women.

"You said for better or for worse."

Harold gazed at his wife, then looked back at his two daughters. He'd have five daughters now. When Zoey came home to visit, he'd live with six women. He turned back to Kelly. "Two daughters." He wiped the tears from her temples with the back of his thumbs. He thought of soft kisses, sweet hugs, and adoring gazes. Daddy's girls. He smiled. "I can't think of anything better than a home full of girls."